DEADLY HARVEST

A
GEORGIA RAE WINSTON
MYSTERY

MARISSA SHROCK

CIMELIAPRESS

Published by Cimelia Press, Greentown, Indiana

Printed in the United States of America

Print ISBN-13: 978-0-9969879-2-9

Library of Congress Control Number: 2018906612

For my grandpas, Jim Shrock and Loren Simpson

For my grandpas, Jim Shrock and Loren Simpson

AUTHOR'S NOTE

One of the best parts of writing a novel is the opportunity to create new places, and this is a power I exercised in *Deadly Harvest*—and in the books to come. However, to give my story an authentic Hoosier feel, I looked to Indiana history to guide me when I named counties, towns, and cities.

Indiana has ninety-two counties, but I added a ninety-third—Richard County—in Central Indiana. My story's county seat, Richardville, is fictional but is named after Jean Baptiste Richardville (1761-1841), an actual Miami chief.

Wildcat Springs is a figment of my imagination but gets its name from Chief Richardville—whose nickname was The Wildcat. The Wildcat Creek really does flow through Central Indiana.

In addition to the liberties I took with Indiana's geography, I used some fictional license with police investigations to remain true to the pace and flow of the story.

CHAPTER ONE

The men were girl talking in the kitchen while the women were watching football in the living room.

I drew a flowered pillow closer to my chest and fidgeted with the gray fringe while I refocused on the TV. Third and inches. The Colts had better not blow it. But the way things were going in my life, what else could I expect?

"Kelsey's awesome." Evan Beckworth's voice drifted in from the kitchen. "I met her parents last weekend."

An invisible hand squeezed my heart when I heard the infatuation in Evan's voice. Or was it love?

"How'd you meet?" my cousin J.T. Simms asked.

"We connected at a tennis tournament this summer. It was like I'd never seen a woman before, you know?"

"Dude, that's awesome."

I rolled my eyes and considered shredding my napkin to make earplugs.

Touchdown. At least something was right in my world. I high-fived my best friend Ashley Choi, who sprawled on the couch next to me.

"Georgia Rae, hand me the chips. I need some salt after that chocolate pie." Ashley made a half-hearted attempt to sit up and wiggle her pale pink fingernails in the direction of the coffee table. I tossed the sack of sour cream and onion chips—her weakness—into her lap.

"Thanks, hon." Ashley tucked a strand of black hair behind her ear, flopped backward, and tore into the bag. She made enough noise to drown out the chitchat in the kitchen and withdrew a handful before daintily popping them in her mouth one at a time.

Kentucky-bred Ashley was always calling people *hon* or *sweetie,* and I'd often wondered how that went over with her fellow engineers, who were mostly male. She was also the only one who called me Georgia Rae without being mad at me.

"How's your grandma?" I asked Ashley, hoping that focusing on someone else's trials would help me block out my own.

Ashley brushed sour-cream-and-onion dust off her hands. "She loves her new knees so much she wants a new hip." She cracked open a can of Diet Coke, took a swig, and set it on the coffee table next to a copy of *Archeology of the Bible.*

"Good. Glad to hear it." I managed a half smile.

"Georgia, are you okay?" Brandi Hartfield's forehead creased as she got up from the other sofa and put a coaster under Ashley's Diet Coke. She was our hostess and my other best friend.

"Yep." I fixed my eyes on the TV. Not here. Not in front of everyone. Out of the corner of my eye, I saw Brandi's curls bob.

She'd pursue this later, which was why Ashley and I sometimes called her *Mom.* Well, that and the fact that she was a good seven years older than me. She hated it when we reminded her, which made it even more fun. Besides, she didn't look older. Not even those nasolabial folds that she obsessed about aged her.

"Is she the one?" J.T. asked Evan. They were still huddled in the kitchen.

What the—*no*. I wasn't going to cuss. Even in my head. God was after me to do better with my mouth, and while I could physically bite my tongue, I was having an awful time in my mind. But really? *The one?* Did guys actually talk like that, or had aliens come along and transplanted Evan's and J.T.'s brains?

Either that or the man bun that J.T. had been sporting lately was infecting his head.

"...can't wait for you guys to meet Kelsey. She's perfect," Evan said. "She couldn't come because of her shift at the hospital, but next time we meet..."

That was swell. *Next time* was at my house. I quickly calculated. In two weeks, I'd probably be done cutting soybeans since we'd already gotten a good start, but the corn might be ready to shell. I could back out of hosting our Bible study and claim exhaustion from harvest.

"Guys, the game's over," Ashley drawled.

The Colts had pulled it off.

J.T. and Evan moseyed into the living room and plopped down on the wood floor. I tried to keep my eyes off of Evan, but I couldn't help stealing a glance. He hadn't shaved for a couple of days, and I loved that look. His sandy hair had just the right amount of wave, and the contours of his muscular chest showed through his Richard County Tennis Tournament T-shirt.

I needed to stop. Right now. Evan was never going to date me, and I needed to accept his relationship with—gag me—twenty-two-year-old Kelsey Lohmann. ASAP. Evan and I were doomed to be just friends, so I'd better figure out a way to be happy for him.

I surveyed the mix of twenty and thirty-somethings gathered in Brandi's living room. Our group was smaller than normal this week because two other members—engaged couple Dave and Heather—were out of town, but the rest of us had decided to meet for a meal and Bible lesson anyway.

Brandi, who was tonight's leader, shut off the TV. "Let's pray before we get started."

Amen to that. I'd need all the prayers I could get.

"Does anybody have any final thoughts on Ecclesiastes?" Brandi asked a half an hour later.

It hadn't been one of our most riveting lessons since it was a wrap-up of the book. Even though Brandi's profession was teaching eighth grade social studies at Wildcat Springs Junior High, she'd struggled to breathe life into this particular study.

I crossed my arms. "Life Lesson #5: Life stinks, is pointless, and then you croak when it's your time. How's that for a final thought?" As soon as the words left my mouth, I thought of Grandma Winston's penchant for spouting life rules and assigning them random numbers.

Grandma lives on. I twisted the amethyst birthstone ring I'd inherited from her a few years ago and observed my friends' reactions.

Ashley covered her mouth with her hand, but her eyes danced. Evan and J.T. exchanged glances.

Evan's hazel eyes filled with concern. "You okay, Georgia? You usually have more to contribute—"

"Peachy. Keepin' it real over here." My cheeks heated. I'd better not be as tomato-y as I felt.

Brandi cleared her throat. "How about any prayer requests or praises?"

Brandi locked her front door behind J.T. and Evan and faced me. She pointed at the shoes in my hand. "Put them down. You're not leaving yet."

I dropped the silver sneakers I'd spent too much money on a few weeks ago. Talking might be good. Besides, Brandi had been through a lot and might have some wisdom.

Ashley's dark eyes widened. "Is something wrong, hon?" She let her pink-striped tote fall from her shoulder onto the floor.

"Really?" Brandi scowled. "How could you not notice? Georgia hardly said a word all evening." She chuckled. "Except for her summary of Ecclesiastes." She sighed. "I can't believe those two guys. I know J.T.'s your cousin, but he's a clueless wonder, and Evan has the sensitivity of a defensive lineman. Coming in here and yammering about some perfect-barely-out-of-diapers girl in front of my best friend."

"Evan doesn't know how I feel about him," I said.

"Why are you defending him? He should know." Brandi marched into the kitchen while Ashley and I trailed behind. "The two of you have been friends for three years, and he's completely oblivious to the fact you care about him." She opened the door to her garage where her Yorkie, Gigi, did a jig in her crate.

Thank you for not using the word love. I tugged my braid when Gigi charged inside, ignored me, and scuttled over to Ashley.

That was the thanks I got for giving Gigi a chew toy for her birthday.

"Brandi's right." Ashley picked up the traitorous dog and stroked her head. "And you can do better than Evan."

"But he's so...hot," I whined. "And godly."

Brandi slammed the back door. "Godly men don't lead women on." Her green eyes flashed as she jerked the slow cooker cord out of the wall and pointed to a cabinet. "Can you get a container for me, please?"

I opened the door to reveal a stack of used butter tubs leaning precariously. As if I were assisting in surgery, I plucked a container and lid out, slapped the door shut, and jumped backward before they could fall.

After handing the container to Brandi, I plopped down at a barstool and leaned my elbows against the island's cool granite. This always happened to me. I'd find a perfect guy and *boom*. He'd meet the love of his life.

I was the ultimate good luck charm.

Guys in search of a wife should line up to be my friend.

Ashley let go of the dog, sat next to me, and draped her arm over my shoulder. "I don't get it, sweetie. You're beautiful. You'll find the right guy soon. We all will."

I snorted. I was honey blond, brown-eyed, and pretty enough —but too tall for my own good. Folks who were kind enough to overlook the few extra pounds I carried had told me for years I should've been a model.

But I'd chosen to be a farmer instead.

And growing up in small-town Indiana right smack dab in the middle of the Central Till Plain, I was living almost every grown man's childhood dream. So, I'd pretty much priced myself right out of a husband here in the good ol' heartland.

Being thirty didn't help either.

"You have a heart of gold, and that's what's most important," Brandi said.

I snorted. "I'd rather have a heart of silver."

"Why?" Brandi inverted the crockpot, and the leftover cocktail wieners slid into the butter tub. Some of the sauce splattered on the counter, and I traced my finger through it.

"Less valuable than gold. That way guys are less likely to steal it." I licked my finger.

Ashley gasped. "Oh, sweetie. You need to see a counselor."

I crossed my arms. "Winstons don't go to therapy."

Brandi put the leftovers in the fridge and scooped up Gigi. "Then you need a pet to cheer you up."

"I have barn cats. And ducks."

Ashley rolled her eyes. "Do the cats even have names?"

I fought a grin. "Uhhh...Stripey and Orangey."

Brandi shook her head. "I meant a dog to keep you company." She turned Gigi toward me and wiggled her paws. "One look at the cute, wittle face, and all your troubles don't seem so bad."

I pointed to the puddle Gigi had deposited on the tile next to the dishwasher. "Seems like *more* trouble to me."

The next day was the perfect afternoon to cut soybeans in our field a few miles outside of my hometown of Wildcat Springs. Not a cloud in the sky, and a hint of crispness in the air. We'd gotten started around one because there'd been heavy dew that morning, and we'd had to wait for the beans to dry out.

Grandpa Winston was driving the tractor and pulling the auger cart while I operated the combine. My perch in the cab offered me a nice view of the countryside that contained mostly farmland crisscrossed by a grid of roads. Every so often, a grove of trees or a house broke up the flat, fertile land.

While I opened up the section of the field next to the road so I'd have room to turn the combine around at the end of each row, Evan and J.T.'s conversation replayed in my head and knifed through my gut.

Why did I care so much? If Evan was truly my friend, then I should be happy he'd met a nice girl. But I didn't need a shrink to tell me I was jealous enough to claw Kelsey's eyes out.

I retrieved a bag of M&Ms from my backpack and ripped

them open with my teeth. I'd start with the chocolate and move to prayer when I got done being mad at God.

Chocolate and prayer—not necessarily in that order—were my therapy. Always had been. Probably always would be.

Truthfully, if I had more prospects, this thing with Evan wouldn't sting as much. But good men were hard to come by. Why couldn't God send a bunch of quality men into my life and let me have a choice instead of waiting around to be chosen? That would be the perfect way to forget all about Evan.

A deluge of men.

I chomped M&Ms and shook my head. I should concentrate. The last thing Grandpa and I needed was a rock coming through the combine header and tearing it up because I was mooning over a guy. Replacing parts took valuable time—and money.

Grandpa was counting on me, and I wasn't going to let him down. When my daddy died almost nine years ago, I'd finished college and come home to help my grandpa with the farm. My brother, Dakota, didn't have any interest. I'd never understood why in heaven's name he'd rather be trapped inside an accounting office crunching numbers all day, but I was thankful because otherwise, I'd be stuck teaching music to a bunch of squirrelly kids. Instead, I got to be out in the sunshine, close to nature.

Okay, that was a teensy bit dramatic. Things were pretty plush in my high-tech, air-conditioned cab with choral music blasting through the speakers. No country music for this gal, thank you very much.

I studied the numbers on the yield monitor, the on-board device I used to keep track of how many bushels we were harvesting per acre. A wet spring and summer had led to repeated flooding, and several gigantic bare spots in our soybean fields meant that yields would be lower than average.

After I made several passes down the field, the grain tank was full. While Grandpa drove the tractor and auger cart alongside the combine, I maneuvered its unloading auger, which looked like a big metal arm, over the cart and dumped the soybeans without stopping. Dumping on the go was more efficient—and Winstons were all about efficiency. Once the auger cart was full, Grandpa would fill the grain truck, and our farmhand Cory would drive the load to the elevator—or store some grain in the bins on my farm so we could sell it later.

Just as I'd finished emptying the load, a rabbit leaped in front of the rotating header and managed to stay ahead of it, scampering for his life. I shrieked and slowed the combine. "Get out of the way, you dumb bunny. Run!"

He didn't scurry fast enough, and the header flipped his body aside.

I squeezed my eyes shut and fought a sob. Seriously? What was wrong with me? PMS? I *never* cried over stuff like this. I hadn't cried since—

"Get a grip, Georgia Rae."

I took a deep breath and let the low rumble of the machinery soothe me. A large wooded area lay ahead, and the trees' leaves displayed yellows, oranges, and reds. As I drew closer, I noticed a lumpy mound protruding from the edge of the woods.

Great. Another dead animal was what I needed today. Probably a deer—which actually wouldn't be the end of the world considering the damage those creatures could do to my crops.

My phone pinged with a text message from Evan.

I need to see you.

Fabulous. Keeping an eye out for rocks, I used one hand to text back.

Busy in field.

9

I shoved more M&Ms in my mouth and prayed he'd get the hint.

I'll come ride along after tennis practice.

"Ugh. Georgia, you stupid bimbo. Why'd you have to go and tell your friends they're welcome in the combine cab any time?"

I didn't have an answer, which was good because it was disturbing enough that I was talking to myself *and* calling myself a bimbo. Putting him off until tomorrow seemed like the best option. Before I could text, I gasped and dropped my phone.

Hitting the brakes, I raised the combine head.

The lump was a human body.

CHAPTER TWO

M y heart thudded as I scrambled out of the cab and down the ladder. I ran around the combine and covered my mouth when I recognized the dark-haired woman sprawled face up next to a log.

Tara Fullerton.

I stepped closer. Flies swarmed Tara's ashen face and indicated there was no need to start CPR. She wore camouflage hunting clothes, and her crossbow rested on the ground a few feet away.

I squeezed my eyes shut.

Back when she was in fifth grade and I was a sophomore in high school, I'd given her piano lessons one summer because her mom had wanted to see if Tara liked playing before she spent a bunch of money on an experienced teacher. Tears stung my eyes as I thought of how excited she'd been to learn to play. But right now, I needed to quit reminiscing and take action.

My phone buzzed, and I swiped to answer the call.

"Grandpa—"

"What's going on over there? Don't tell me you hit a rock."

I opened my mouth to speak, but the words died in my throat. "A body." I managed to rasp the words.

"A what? Speak up."

I cleared my throat and blinked back the tears blurring my vision. "I found Tara Fullerton—dead."

Grandpa swore. "I'm comin'. Call 911." He disconnected, and his tractor moved across the field along the path I'd harvested.

My fingers shook as I tapped in the numbers.

"Nine-one-one. What's your emergency?"

"I was cutting beans and found a body in the woods at the edge of my field. I'm a farmer." *Way to state the obvious.* I knelt beside the form. "A dead body. A young woman. Her name is Tara Fullerton." I tugged on my braid and adjusted my baseball cap as I looked around. My eyes landed on my daddy's permanent tree stand about twenty feet above where Tara lay.

"You're certain the victim is dead."

"Yes, ma'am. There's no question. Looks like she took a fall from a tree stand." I squeezed my eyes shut, pushing away unwelcome memories that threatened to surface.

Stay focused.

"What's your location?"

I turned from Tara, gave the dispatcher our address, promised not to touch the body—like that was even an option—and disconnected. Grandpa pulled up and scurried out of the tractor. He moved pretty quickly for a seventy-seven-year-old.

He removed his baseball cap and pressed it against his chest as he approached. "Poor thing." He rubbed his bald head as he surveyed the scene.

Her family's lives would be changed forever. Did Tara have a husband or boyfriend? I'd lost track of her after I'd gone to college.

Lord, comfort Tara's loved ones.

"You give her permission to hunt back here?" He put his hat back on. "'Cause I sure didn't."

I pulled my gaze from the body and concentrated on his question. "No. And that's weird because Tara knows—knew—me, so she could've just asked."

"Maybe she thought it'd be better to ask forgiveness than permission," Grandpa said.

"Probably." A lump formed in my throat as I studied the simple ladder and wide, wooden platform that Daddy'd built years ago. I'd gone hunting with him one time and could picture the two of us huddled on the stand. I'd been about thirteen. When we'd spotted a doe, I'd gasped, and she'd darted away.

Daddy hadn't said a word, but he'd never taken me again. Shaking off the pain, I refocused on the present. "I swore we wouldn't touch the body, but I didn't promise we wouldn't check out the woods." I needed to think about something—anything—other than Tara.

"Whaddya think you're gonna find?"

"I'm not sure, but I want to know where she parked, because I didn't see her car earlier." I stepped into the tree line, and Grandpa joined me. I was probably creeped out from finding a body, but something didn't feel right. Was it because Tara had been hunting alone? Most women I knew hunted with a family member or boyfriend. She could've liked the alone time, but Tara had always seemed social.

A twig cracked, and I shrieked.

"Georgia Rae Winston, calm down, or the sheriff's gonna find two bodies when he gets here."

Grandpa had survived a heart attack twenty years earlier and had fought to stay healthy ever since—even though his heart wasn't strong. "Sorry." My own heart chugged and didn't show signs of slowing down.

We crept further into the woods, but nothing appeared out of the ordinary. Fallen leaves crunched under our feet, and moss-covered logs crisscrossed a carpet of twigs and leaves. A squirrel scampered up a tree. Field dust sparkled in the air where the sun peeked through the trees.

We kept going, and I spotted a dark blue sedan. When I approached the car, I stopped. The tree line jutted out in front of the tiny grass clearing where she'd parked, which helped block the view of her car from the road—and from the section of the field we'd harvested so far.

It was probably nothing—just my suspicious mind at work. Besides, she'd been hunting out here without permission, so she'd probably parked that way hoping we wouldn't notice. I cupped my hands around my face and peered through the windows—without touching, of course.

All the door locks were pushed down, but the keys dangled from the ignition.

A phone, which I assumed belonged to Tara, rested on the passenger's seat. Two travel mugs sat in the cup holders. Had someone been hunting with Tara?

Maybe that person had gone to get help since the keys were locked in the car. But shouldn't Tara's hunting buddy have been back by now? I didn't know much about corpses, but she'd been dead for at least a few hours.

Or the explanation was much simpler. She'd been hunting alone, accidentally locked her keys in the car, and let her own dirty mugs pile up.

"I reckon we'd better get out of here before we mess up something we didn't aim to," Grandpa said. "The sheriff's department can handle any investigating."

"I suppose." Not to mention, experience had taught me I was no Jessica Fletcher.

When the sheriff and several deputies arrived, Grandpa and I moved the combine and tractor out of the way and stood watching the action from a distance while the investigators swarmed around the edge of the field and entered the woods.

Sheriff Anderson ambled over to our post and shook Grandpa's hand. "Good to see you again, Ron. When are you planning on retiring?"

"Don't believe in retirement," Grandpa said. "Work keeps a man young."

"Not in my business. When my term's up, I'll be spending plenty of time with my wife at our cabin down in the Smoky Mountains. Hey, did I ever tell you—"

"When will you know for sure if this is an accident or not?" I asked.

Sheriff Anderson raised a bushy eyebrow. "I'm sure the autopsy'll confirm this was an accident."

"Right." My cheeks burned. This wasn't an episode of *Psych*, so I needed to stop looking for clues like my favorite TV detective, Shawn Spencer and his sidekick, Burton "Gus" Guster.

"It's a shame. Falls from tree stands cause more deaths than hunters accidently getting shot." He shook his head. "She should've had on a safety harness."

Grandpa adjusted his baseball cap. "Not to sound insensitive, but she was trespassing. We sure didn't give her permission to hunt out here."

Sheriff Anderson nodded. "Good to know."

"Do you think it's weird she was hunting alone?" I put my hands on my hips.

Sheriff Anderson sighed and did a poor job of covering the annoyance that flickered in his expression. "No. Some people like their space. *If* there's anything that indicates foul play, which I'm not saying there is, we'll find it."

I had my doubts about that.

"Look," Sheriff Anderson said, "I know you've got to go on with harvesting while the weather's cooperating, so after we get your statements, if you want to move across the road to your other field, you won't bother us. It'll be a while before we clear this area, though."

"We understand." Grandpa extended his hand. "Keep us posted, and let me know if there's any other way I can help."

Sheriff Anderson gazed over at the investigators. "I sure appreciate it."

"Georgia!" Evan jumped out of his silver Accord that he'd parked in the grass on the side of the road. "What's going on?"

I'd forgotten to answer his text, but he'd remembered where I said we'd be harvesting and had shown up anyway.

Fantastic.

I ran my fingers over my hair to get rid of soybean particles but couldn't do anything about the black smudge of grease adorning my sweatshirt. *So attractive.*

Evan jogged over to where Grandpa and I stood watching the action from across the road. We couldn't bring ourselves to get back to work. A reporter from the *Richard County Gazette* had arrived and started talking to Sheriff Anderson. I prayed he wouldn't realize I'd been the one to discover the body because I had zero intention of talking to the media.

Concern creased Evan's brow as he moved his sunglasses to the top of his head. He was wearing black athletic shorts and a gray T-shirt with a blue, pouncing wildcat. "Are you two okay?"

"Sort of." I dug my boot toe into the dirt while I told him what had happened.

"Holy cow." He gave me a hug. "That poor girl."

"Yeah." I swallowed and tried not to think about how Tara's

family and friends would feel when they found out, but the thought kept pinging in my brain, making my stomach churn. I hitched my thumb toward the combine. "We were just ready to get back to work."

"I'll come back another time."

I started to agree that would be best, but the kindness in his eyes stopped me. "No. You can stay." It might be nice to have a friend around for a distraction.

I caught Grandpa's gaze as he turned to go back to his tractor, and his eyes twinkled.

Evan and I climbed in the combine cab. Thank goodness for GPS and autosteer because without it, I wouldn't be able to keep the combine in a straight line with Evan sitting in the instructional seat next to me.

Keep the conversation light. "How was practice?" Evan coached varsity tennis at Wildcat Springs High School where he was also the guidance counselor.

"Good. Although we'll get drilled in the regional this week." He shrugged. "I'm proud of the guys for winning our sectional, though." He watched as I started the combine. "Do you need to talk about finding the body?"

Yes. Not really. "I'm fine. Or I will be once I get the mental picture out of my mind." I swallowed. "Tara's life was important, you know? Someone's going to be devastated that she's gone."

"You certainly understand that."

"Right." I clamped my mouth shut. "What brings you by?"

His forehead creased with concern. "If you don't want to talk about this stuff with me, I can refer you to a great Christian counselor."

Why did everyone keep insisting that I should talk to a shrink?

"Thanks. I appreciate it." I flipped my braid over my shoulder and glanced at the yield monitor. The beans' moisture level was perfect—so at least *something* was going right. "What's on your mind? From what I overheard last night, things are going great with Kelsey." Might as well get it out in the open, so he was aware that I knew.

"Yeah, she's great." He cleared his throat. "That's actually what I wanted to talk to you about, but obviously now's not the best time."

To tell the truth, I didn't know what I'd thought Evan wanted when he'd texted me earlier. Finding Tara had distracted me from acknowledging that deep down I'd been hoping he was telling me he'd come to his senses, dumped Kelsey, and realized I was the one for him.

I needed to pretend like that thought had never entered the deepest, darkest cranny of my mind. *Remember your acting skills, Georgia.* "Why?" My voice was pitched a tad too high to sound natural.

"Georgia, you don't have to play tough for me. That conversation had to be hard to hear. If I could've shut J.T. up, I would've, but you know how he is. The guy has the tenacity of a bulldog."

That wasn't how I'd describe my laid-back cousin, but whatever. "I'm confused," I said. "What was hard to hear?"

Evan's brow furrowed. "About Kelsey and me."

I studied the combine head chopping up the soybeans and thought of the dead rabbit. That's how I felt. Flipped aside by a piece of machinery that'd invaded my space. I raised my chin. "Why would that be so hard?" I wanted to make him say it.

"Because of our history."

I wasn't sure *history* was the right word because that implied there'd been a romantic relationship—instead of an awkward friendship. For the second time that day, a lump grew in my throat. How much trauma was one girl supposed to deal with in a matter of a few hours?

Not fair, God.

I'd deal with God later. Evan was studying me as if I might snap at any second, so I had to say something. "Look, Evan. It's best that you and I remain just friends. If you're happy with Kelsey, I'm thrilled for you." My heart had a different opinion, but my head was on board.

"But you seemed upset last night."

Why hadn't I done a better job of hiding my feelings? I shifted. "Not for the reasons you think." I sighed and picked a hangnail. "See, I had a lousy blind date on Saturday night." I wasn't lying, so I didn't need to add that to my list of sins to confess, because the collection of pent up cuss words pinging around my head was large enough to fill a football stadium. "It's frustrating to see things working out for other people while you're stuck having the same bad date over and over again."

I'd made it sound like I had lots of dates. The truth? Saturday night's outing had been my first in a while, and the dude had been a real tool. In addition to his entrée, he had insisted on ordering three beers for himself, an appetizer, and dessert that I'd eaten one bite of before he instructed the waiter to split our check. In half. While I'd been in the restroom.

Evan's shoulders sagged. "I was afraid I'd hurt you. That's the last thing I want to do because I care about our friendship."

I winced inwardly. "I know."

"So we're good?"

Why did it matter so much to him? "Yep. Now hang on. I've got to concentrate while I dump this load, and then I want you to tell me all about Kelsey."

He beamed. "Great."

My heart kicked in protest. I grabbed the bag of M&M's and held them out to Evan. When he shook his head, I dumped the remaining candies in my hand and shoved them in my mouth.

Help me, Lord.

CHAPTER THREE

Tuesday morning, clad in my flannel, frog-print jammies, I stumbled out of my bedroom and into the living room where I turned on the TV for the morning news. "...the Richard County Sheriff's Department has identified the victim as twenty-five-year-old Tara Fullerton, who died due to injuries sustained during a fall from a tree stand. Sheriff Andy Anderson says this incident is a sobering reminder that all hunters should wear safety harnesses while hunting in tree stands."

I waited for more information, but the anchor moved on to the next story. Biting my lip, I shuffled into my 1980's era kitchen that begged for an update to its linoleum flooring and pastel flower-basket print wallpaper. I'd purchased the one-hundred-year-old farmhouse where I'd grown up from my mom when she'd remarried, and because the whole place was in need of updating, she'd given me a good deal.

The two-story home boasted a huge front porch, original woodwork, and a staircase that added the type of character designers on TV were always raving about. Though it was too much house for me right now, I hoped someday I'd be able to have children who'd help bring the place back to life—like it'd been when Dakota and I were kids.

After I started a pot of coffee, my eyes fell on the stack of dirty dishes in the sink. I'd tackle them after coffee. My dishwasher had quit working, and I hadn't had time to see if Grandpa and I could resurrect it.

While I opened the pantry door, walked inside, and grabbed a box of Cinnamon Toast Crunch, my mind wandered to Tara. Today she was simply a cautionary tale that would be forgotten at the end of a news cycle, but she was more than that. I poured the remaining cereal in a bowl, chucked the empty box in the trash, and looked in my refrigerator for milk—which I didn't have.

Dry cereal it is.

Why couldn't the newscasters have shared something personal about Tara's life? I sat at the kitchen table and opened my laptop, hoping to learn more about the adult version of Tara. While I ate, I started with Facebook and Instagram.

Perusing Tara's pages revealed several things. The first was that she should've had better privacy settings. The second was that she often worked out at Fitness Universe in the nearby city of Richardville. Third? She was dating Mike Dunson, and there were plenty of vomit-inducing selfies to prove it.

It seemed strange that her profiles didn't mention hunting. Most female hunters I knew weren't afraid to brag about it because that hobby was pretty impressive to some guys. Tara had grown up with a single mom, and she hadn't had a father to teach her the necessary skills. Which meant at some point, she'd probably had a boyfriend who'd shown her—maybe even her current boyfriend. If so, then why had she been hunting alone?

Or her fall hadn't been accidental, and her hunting buddy had fled the scene.

No. I needed to stop with the questions and speculation. Sheriff Anderson's disgusted expression when I'd asked about foul play loomed in my mind as I got up and poured coffee into my favorite owl-shaped mug. Perhaps Tara had recently started a new hobby. I shouldn't let my past experiences cause me to make assumptions, because Heaven knew I didn't need to go and irritate the sheriff's department—again.

Grandpa, Cory, and I survived an exhausting—and mercifully distracting—four days of harvesting beans, including the field where I'd found Tara's body. Saturday afternoon brought rain, so after a nap, I sat down at my kitchen table, where I'd stacked mail for the last several days. I made quick work of separating bills from junk mail, but a pale blue envelope with a P.O. box return address—but no name—caught my attention. Probably another invitation to a baby shower. I certainly received my fair share of those since most of my childhood friends had married several years ago and were onto the baby-making phase of life.

I ripped open the envelope and pulled out a blue and white striped card covered in neat print on the inside.

Dear Georgia,

I hope this note finds you well. I have awesome memories of taking piano lessons from you. This is going to sound weird, but I could use some investigation advice, and I don't want to involve the police yet. I also don't have the money to hire a PI. Bobbi Sue Miller told me you've never given up on finding answers in your dad's case, and with all of your experience, you might be able to give me some insight on my situation.

I'm pretty scared, so I didn't want to risk contacting you by email, phone, or social media. If you're willing to meet, I'll be at Latte Conspiracies in Wildcat Springs on Thursday, October 5, from 6:00 until closing. Feel free to stop by any time. I hope to see you there.

 Sincerely,
 Tara Fullerton

The note fell out of my hand and plunked onto the table as blood pulsed in my head and my gut clenched. It wasn't only the shock of getting a note from Tara. That was bad enough, but one line in her note mocked me: *You've never given up on finding answers in your dad's case.*

But I had.

Daddy's murder investigation had gone cold, and in spite of the sheriff's department's best efforts—and my private quest for answers—nobody had been able to explain why one of Wildcat Springs's most beloved citizens had been shot and killed one October night on his way home from a school board meeting, where he'd served as president.

Detectives theorized he'd spotted suspicious activity at the grain elevator a few miles from our house. When he stopped to look, he'd stumbled on a robbery in progress and had been shot before he could call 911. But the lack of evidence and security cameras had made it difficult to solve the case.

I'd abandoned all investigative efforts three years ago. Apparently, Bobbi Sue hadn't gotten the memo. I rested my head in my hands.

Wait a second. I lifted my head.

If Tara was too scared to go to the police, then my gut feeling was right, and her death wasn't an accident. I had to turn in the note.

I scrolled through my phone, located the number for the sheriff's department, and tapped the call button.

"I need to speak with the person in charge of the Tara

Fullerton investigation," I said when a woman with a nasal voice answered.

"That'd be Detective Perkins. I'll put you through to his voicemail."

Voicemail. Of course. It was Saturday evening. While the detective's greeting played, I tried to gather my thoughts to overcome the hurdle of leaving a coherent message.

"Detective Perkins, this is Georgia Winston. I need to talk to you about a note I received from Tara Fullerton. It sounds like she was in trouble before she died." I left my number and disconnected. As soon as I ended the call, my phone vibrated with a text from Ashley.

Where r u? Dinner's almost ready.

Right. Dinner with Ashley and Brandi. With my churning stomach, eating would be impossible. I glanced down at my thighs. Well, probably not as impossible as I wanted to believe. My jeans were snug, thanks to a lack of exercise during the last few weeks. I picked up my phone and texted back.

On my way.

I folded Tara's note so that the print showed, slid it in a plastic bag, and began a search for my purse and shoes.

It wasn't unusual for Brandi, Ashley, and me to gather for dinner and a movie on a Saturday night when none of us had dates—which was far more often than either Ashley or I liked to admit. Both Ashley and Brandi could cook—and were good at it—so they nearly always made a meal. I'd missed out on the culinary gene when God was handing out domestic talents, so my idea of cooking was ordering wings or pizza from the local joint, but my friends never seemed to mind.

"Hon, I'm making good old southern comfort food tonight," Ashley said as I walked in the back door of her newly renovated 1920's bungalow. From her front porch, she had a view of Sycamore Park, and she lived within walking distance of our favorite coffee shop and her favorite bookstore.

Ashley was working at the marble-topped island, and she wore a cupcake print apron trimmed in pink. "I figured you'd need the good stuff after the week you've had."

Brandi and Ashley didn't know the half of it since I hadn't bothered to fill them in about Evan. "Sounds perfect." My tone didn't make it to enthusiastic and died somewhere around lackadaisical. I dropped down on the bench in the breakfast nook.

Brandi's forehead creased as she walked to the refrigerator and began filling glasses with water. "Something's bothering you. Besides finding Tara."

"Yeah." I recounted my awkward conversation with Evan in the combine cab while Brandi and Ashley gaped at me.

"Unbelievable." Ashley dumped an eight-ounce container of sour cream into steaming potatoes and started smashing. "I'm pretending these potatoes are Evan's—"

"Ashley Marie Choi." Brandi stopped filling a glass with water.

Ashley's neck grew blotchy, and she whirled toward the refrigerator, wielding the hand masher as a weapon. Globs of potatoes dripped onto the blue and white patterned tile. "What on earth did you think I was going to say, *Mom?*" She raised her chin. "I was going to say head." She turned around and slammed the hand masher with gusto.

I smiled, got up, and wiped the potatoes off the floor.

Brandi's face melted into a scowl. "Can you believe the arrogance of that guy?"

"He was trying to be sensitive." I washed the potatoes off my hands and cleaned the spot on the floor with a wet paper towel. "Besides, he knew it wasn't the best time. I goaded him into telling me."

"He also showed up without an invitation," Brandi said.

"Technically, you all have an open invitation to the combine cab."

"And this city girl needs to take you up on that because it sounds completely fascinating, and it might impress a few men I know." Ashley finished the potatoes and dropped the masher in the sink. "By the way, you shouldn't defend Evan. As far as I'm concerned, he was trying to ease his own conscience because he knows he led you on."

That pretty much summed it up, since his little visit had removed all doubt that he'd known how I felt about him. "It's fine. Believe me, there're bigger problems in the world."

"No, it's not fine." Brandi picked up the stack of silverware from the counter and began placing it around the table in the dining room. "None of this is, and you don't have to pretend with us."

My throat thickened. "Thanks. But you know what? Let's talk about someone else's issues right now. I'm tired of thinking about my own." I stole a crouton from the salad bowl on the island. "Like how about when *you're* going to go on a date, Brandi." I popped the crouton in my mouth and crunched.

Her eyes darkened. "I'm not ready."

"But it's been almost three years," I said. Brandi's husband Brian had died in a car accident.

"Your blind date stories don't exactly inspire me to reenter the dating pool." She grinned and fiddled with the silverware.

"You have to admit they're funny. Don't you want fodder to entertain us with?"

"Now, ladies. How would these poor gentlemen feel if they knew we were laughing at their expense?" Ashley removed fried chicken that'd been warming in the oven.

"Like they never laugh at us." My phone vibrated in my purse, and I prayed it was the detective. "Excuse me." I walked through the dining room and into the living room where I answered.

"Detective Cal Perkins, returning your call."

I pushed aside the teal decorative pillows, perched on Ashley's couch with my back to my friends, and tried to remember if I'd met Detective Perkins the day I'd found the body. Detective Marvin Kimball had taken my statement, and this man's pleasant, resonant voice was a nice contrast to Detective Kimball's smoker's growl.

"Ms. Winston? Are you there?"

"Yes, sir," I whispered and then cleared my throat. "I received a letter from Tara Fullerton today. She asked me to meet her this past Thursday because she was having some sort of trouble and needed my advice. She was scared and didn't want to involve the police."

"The letter came today? And she wanted advice from *you*?" There was no mistaking the skepticism in his tone.

"I *opened* it today. I don't know what day it came. See, I'm a farmer, and I was in the middle of cutting beans, and I let my mail pile up, so I just got to it today. I used to give Tara piano lessons, and—"

"Ms. Winston, take a breath and tell me why you think Tara Fullerton wanted to speak with you."

I did and rested my elbows on my knees. "I'm sorry. Finding her body and getting this letter have brought back memories of my daddy's murder. His case went cold, and for years everybody in Wildcat Springs knew I was investigating, and that's why Bobbi Sue from Latte Conspiracies told Tara about me, but Bobbi Sue doesn't know I gave up three years ago because I never found any answers, and I don't know why she ever thought I'd be able to help Tara in the first—"

"Ms. Winston, take another breath."

"I'm sorry for babbling." I clenched my fist. "I'm the one who found Tara Fullerton's body. In my field. That I own." I said the words to try to make myself sound respectable, but it was probably way too late for that since I was coming off like I belonged in a loony bin.

"I know. Tell you what," he said as if he were trying to pacify me. "Bring that letter into the sheriff's department Monday morning around nine, and we'll talk."

"I will. Thank you, sir." I disconnected and stared at Ashley's coffee table that her mother had brought from Korea when she'd moved to the United States years ago. I wanted to fly away like the mother-of-pearl birds in the design.

"Georgia?" Brandi's eyes widened when she saw me. Wiping her hands on her jeans, she sat next to me. "What's going on? Was that Evan? Because if he's upset you again, I'll—"

I swallowed, pulled the bagged note out of my purse, and handed it to her.

She sat next to me, read it, and gasped. "This is disturbing."

"I was talking to a detective about it." I rested my head in my hands. "Why would Bobbi Sue think I could help Tara when I never even figured out who killed my dad?"

"Hold the phone." Ashley walked in. "Did I hear you say someone *killed* your dad?" She untied her apron and threw it on the rocking chair next to the couch.

"Yeah. And they never caught the murderer."

"I'm so sorry, hon." Tears filled Ashley's eyes as she knelt beside me. "You never told me that's how he died." There wasn't an ounce of accusation in her voice—just shock.

"I don't like to talk about it." I laced my fingers and squeezed. It surprised me that she'd lived in Wildcat Springs for two and a half years and hadn't heard. Had people already forgotten my daddy?

"That's understandable." Ashley brushed her hand across her eyes.

Brandi put her arm around me. "Let's pray about this. Right now."

She thought prayer solved everything, which I guess I should believe too, but I'd never quite gotten to that point. It always impressed me that she actually had—considering everything she'd endured.

"Yes, let's do it." Ashley clasped my hand.

I nodded.

"Father, we're scared and confused," Brandi said. "We don't understand why Georgia's dad died, but please bring the person responsible to justice. Give Georgia peace and hope. Show us how to help. Help the authorities figure out what happened to Tara. Amen."

I took a shuddering breath and lifted my head. "We should eat. There's no point in letting Ashley's good food go to waste."

As we stood, I didn't miss the fact that Ashley and Brandi exchanged worried glances. But I didn't care. I'd been dealing with this longer than we'd been friends and was a professional at handling it.

That night, I couldn't sleep, so I settled into my daddy's black leather recliner that occupied the same space in front of the fireplace that it had when this house had belonged to my parents.

During the day, I could look out at the pond and my vegetable patch and remember all the years daddy and I had spent tending the garden.

I tucked the black and white blanket my late grandma Winston had crocheted around my legs and lifted the footrest. Opening my laptop, I found the file labeled *Murder Investigation*.

I'd given up because my search for answers had robbed me of joy. When God had asked me to let it go, I'd obeyed, though it had been one of the hardest things I'd ever done. I thought of my small group's recent Bible study in Ecclesiastes, and one verse from chapter three came to mind.

"A time to search and a time to give up."

God cared about justice. Would he allow Daddy's case to go unsolved forever?

What are you doing, Lord? Do you want me to start searching for answers again?

Blinking moisture from my eyes, I studied the document with notes and observations from my research that were all dead ends. With a sigh, I slapped the laptop shut and stared at the family pictures on the mantle. My favorite was the one of Daddy and me that Mom had taken in front of our old red barn the Father's Day before his murder.

Life had seemed so much simpler then. Right now, I didn't have any answers.

About anything.

CHAPTER FOUR

"Georgia!" Beverly Alspaugh stopped and grasped my arm. Fellow churchgoers at Wildcat Springs Community Church milled around us in the multi-purpose room during the fellowship time between Sunday school and the main service. Clusters of people stood sipping lattes, mochas, or plain old dark roast coffee they'd purchased from the shop in the corner. All the proceeds went to an orphanage in Guatemala.

"I'm so glad I caught you." Beverly adjusted her floral-print blouse.

I gave her a quick hug. "How're you feeling?"

"About the same. Cancer's relentless, but I'm not giving up." She patted her curly gray wig.

"I'll keep praying." I wasn't good with remembering to ask God about every little thing, but I did keep the weekly list of church requests on my refrigerator—and Beverly was at the top of it. Had been for a year.

"Thank you, dear. Enough about that." She clutched my arm. "I've been meaning to call you because you had a rotten week. I can't imagine how horrifying it must've been to find the Fullerton girl in your field."

"Be glad you can't imagine it." It was a picture that'd never leave my mind.

"Oh, mercy!" Beverly covered her red lips with her arthritis-bent fingers. "I've been praying for everyone involved since I heard, but that isn't why I stopped you."

My radar pinged, and I glanced around in search of Brandi, Ashley, or any one of my other friends who'd chosen that moment to migrate to Siberia.

There were only a couple of reasons the older ladies in the church stopped me. Grandpa used to be one, but he was currently off the market in a relationship with Wanda Morris, a sweet widow he'd known since high school.

That left the other reason. *Wait for it...*

"How's your love life?"

And there it was. "Well, I—"

"Have you tried online dating? My granddaughter met her husband that way. They're as happy as can be and are expecting my first great-grandbaby. You know, lots of young ladies meet gentlemen that way."

I wouldn't use the word *gentlemen* to describe some of the men I'd met online, though in fairness—and Winstons were fair—there were a few good men like Evan out there, roaming the dating-world forest like rare beasts that huntresses paid for the privilege to stalk. I'd even encountered one or two who'd escaped capture. "I've already—"

"There's no shame in it. And if you're careful, it can be a fantastic opportunity." She took a breath, and I opened my mouth, but she blazed ahead. "But that's not what I wanted to talk to you about, because I have a better idea."

"Really?"

She leaned forward conspiratorially. "My great-nephew just

moved to town, and I'd like you to help welcome him." She winked. "I'll invite him to church, and you take care of the rest. There're lots of single girls around this church, but you're the perfect one for him. He's a good man who's looking for a Christian wife. He's even tall."

"And how would he feel about a Christian wife who's a farmer?"

"Good heavens." She waved. "He's a modern young man. Your profession won't put him off. By the way, he was a major league pitcher for two years."

Very interesting. "What team?"

"Texas Rangers."

I smiled. "I'd be happy to meet him. He could even join my small group—it's a mix of guys and girls."

"Oh, that's perfect. Thank you. I know you'll make him feel right at home." Beverly peeked around my shoulder. "Excuse me, dear. I need to talk to Mary Ann." She slipped by me.

"Wait, what's his name?"

But she was already engrossed in conversation with Mary Ann.

Monday morning, rain drove against my truck's windshield, a reminder that harvest had been delayed. But, I didn't panic since we were done cutting beans. As soon as the fields dried, we'd start shelling corn.

While I drove to the Richard County Sheriff's Department, located in the county seat of Richardville, I fought the memory of the deputy who'd shown up at our front door that October evening when I'd been home from college for fall break. I'd padded downstairs in my flannel pajamas to see what the commotion was about. Mom had been wearing her hunter green robe.

As soon as I'd seen the man in the brown and tan uniform and processed the mix of pain and sympathy displayed on his face, I'd known.

Daddy wasn't late getting home. He was gone.

I shook my head to shoo away the recollection and parked. The rain diminished to a thin drizzle that misted my face and dotted my coat with water droplets as I walked toward the limestone building.

I entered a small waiting area that contained a few black plastic chairs pushed against a grimy gray wall, and a receptionist who was twenty-five-ish opened a glass window. "May I help you?" She flipped her bangs out of her eyes.

"I'd like to speak with Detective Perkins, please."

"Do you have an appointment?" She arched her overly tweezed eyebrows as if she didn't believe I did.

"Yes. Georgia Winston."

She pursed her lips. "I'll let him know you're here."

As I waited, I studied the pictures of meth users—before and after—which someone had posted on the wall. I cringed at the damage that drug inflicted. Missing teeth and premature aging plagued every person.

"Horrifying, aren't they?"

I blinked at the receptionist who seemed amused by my revulsion. "Yes, *ma'am*."

Her eyes narrowed at my use of *ma'am*, and I fought a smirk. I really should be nicer.

The sound of someone whistling the theme song from *Castle* filtered into the waiting area. The door swung open, and a dark-haired man who I guessed was in his late thirties smiled—and my heart dinged.

Just a little.

I'd never known it was possible for a man to make me feel petite, but when I looked up into his handsome face, I was immensely thankful that such a possibility actually existed. I'd have to check for a wedding ring when it wouldn't be obvious. Had I been so distracted that I hadn't noticed this gorgeous man at the crime scene?

Good grief, Georgia Rae. No wonder you're single.

"Come on back, Ms. Winston." He flashed a smile, and a dimple appeared and vanished.

A dimple. "It's Miss. Not Ms." *How subtle.* "Because I'm *not* a feminist." *Really helpful.*

When he stopped and faced me, his blue eyes danced. "Noted." He led me through a maze of desks to his workspace with a computer, piles of file folders, several mugs, and a crumpled bag from Latte Conspiracies. He pointed to the seat at the side of his desk, and I caught sight of the nameplate as I eased into the chair and faced him. *Detective Calvin Perkins.*

And no wedding ring.

My glee over that discovery dropped dead. It didn't matter if he was single or not since I'd blown any chance I might've had by sounding like a crazy lady on the phone Saturday night. I busied myself by removing the baggie with Tara's note from my purse and handing it to Detective Perkins. "I know I sounded nuts when we talked on the phone. I'm quite sane. I just wanted to report the note in case it ended up being important."

He took a seat, faced me, and studied the note. "Thanks for bagging this. Are you the only one who touched it?"

I lifted my chin. "Yes." *Fine. Don't meet me halfway. Assume I'm crazy.*

He met my gaze. "I talked to Bobbi Sue at Latte Conspiracies this morning to see if she had any idea what Tara needed help with and why she directed her to you."

Maybe since he'd spoken to Bobbi Sue, he didn't think I was nuts after all. Either that or he'd been trying to figure out if he had an appointment with a whacko. I leaned forward. "And?"

He tapped the note. "This confirms what Bobbi Sue told me. Tara was a regular who bent Bobbi Sue's ear on occasion. A couple of weeks ago Tara told Bobbi Sue she didn't have the money or desire to hire a private investigator, so Bobbi Sue mentioned you because of the work you did on your dad's case."

Even though I was thankful the note was legitimate, I rolled my eyes. "It's not like I'm an amateur sleuth." Although I'd probably watched enough murder mysteries on TV to qualify.

"I know."

I searched for any sign of levity in his inscrutable expression. None. I crossed my arms. Had he been making fun of me by whistling *Castle*'s theme song? "You don't have to be so quick to agree. I'm aware I've failed at finding my dad's killer—but so has this department."

He cleared his throat. "I asked Bobbi Sue why she didn't counsel Tara to come to us, and she didn't give me a straight answer."

"That's easy." I shrugged. "Everybody in Wildcat Springs knows Bobbi Sue doesn't trust cops. Her dad did time for a crime he didn't commit because someone framed him."

He cocked an eyebrow. "I see." He'd resorted to his skeptical tone.

"Seriously. Her dad was exonerated." I motioned to his computer. "Look it up sometime."

"Her coffee shop makes sense now." He picked up the cup from Latte Conspiracies that had an alien printed on it.

"Right." I clutched my purse handle. "I don't suppose Bobbi Sue knew what Tara's problem was?"

"Nope."

I wasn't sure if he was telling the truth. It didn't matter. I'd talk to Bobbi Sue myself.

Detective Perkins leaned back and steepled his fingers. "How often did you see Tara after you stopped giving her piano lessons?"

"Not often because we didn't keep in touch." I chewed my lower lip. "She visited my church a few months ago, and we spoke briefly. It was the first time I'd seen her in probably five years."

"Wildcat Springs Community Church?"

"Yes." I tilted my head. "How'd you know?"

His dimple made a comeback. "Aunt Beverly said when I visited that church, I should be on the lookout for Georgia Winston."

Sweet baby Moses in a basket.

My face and neck grew warm. "It's funny because when Beverly told me about you, we were interrupted, and she never got around to telling me your name." I let out a nervous chuckle. "What a coincidence."

"Sure is." He took a sip of coffee, but his eyes sparkled with amusement and made me squirm. He'd been toying with me the whole time.

Time to get out of here.

I stood. "If you need anything else, please give me a call." Why had I said *anything*? Would he misinterpret my statement as flirting? If he did, maybe he'd be flattered instead of repulsed.

"Miss Winston, there's something else I'd like to talk to you about." He motioned to the chair.

I sat and pulled my purse to my chest.

He leaned forward, folded his hands, and rested them on his desk. "I'm reviewing your dad's case. I'm hoping to bring a different perspective."

I blew out a breath. "Thank you." I shook my head. "I put so much time into investigating that it made my life miserable, and I had to stop."

"I have a heart for cold cases because families need closure." Sincerity shone in his eyes.

"You don't know how much this means to me—and my family."

"Let me get some answers before you're too grateful."

"Fair enough."

"Georgia Winston!" Bobbi Sue Miller smacked the stainless-steel counter as soon as I walked into Latte Conspiracies with the intent of satisfying my curiosity—and need for more caffeine. "Look at you, girl. You get prettier every time I see you. Why aren't you married yet?"

Never had a snappy comeback for that one. "I like your *Star Wars* shirt."

She glanced down at Princess Leia and thrust out her chest. "The hubs got this for my birthday. Can you believe I hit the big 5-o this year?"

"I thought you were twenty-nine." I winked.

She snorted. "You're full of it, like your daddy was. What can I get you?"

I studied the individual clipboards that hung above the counter and displayed the names of the specialty drinks. The Area 51 was my usual, but I was in the mood for something different than a vanilla latte with a dash of cinnamon. "A large Moon Landing Mocha, and the answer to a question." I glanced around the shop, from the concrete floors to the exposed duct-work, that gave the place its industrial vibe. The early morning rush had subsided, and a few customers with laptops sat at the wood and metal tables scattered around. To my left, an opening led to Miller's Books, which Bobbi Sue's husband Hemingway ran—like his mother before him. I never spent time in the bookstore because reading wasn't my thing.

Bobbi Sue took my money and punched my loyalty card. "You're here about the Fullerton girl, aren't you?" She handed me the card. One more purchase until my freebie.

"She sent me a note. I got it on Saturday." I tucked the card in my wallet for safekeeping.

Bobbi Sue's eyes widened. "I bet that gave you a jolt, getting a message from the grave." She began steaming milk.

"Well, she sent it before she died."

"You sure about that?" Bobbi Sue poured the milk into a cup.

I choked back a laugh. "I didn't check the postmark."

She looked triumphant as she popped the lid on my drink.

I'd give her the win if I could learn what Tara wanted. "Do you know what Tara's problem was?"

She handed me the mocha. "I didn't tell that handsome detective everything I knew." She took a rag from her apron pocket and rubbed the counter as if wiping away fingerprints could erase her guilt. "By the way, you ought to go out with him if he doesn't have a girlfriend. I bet he doesn't because he's in here by himself an awful lot."

"Bobbi Sue, he's a cop." I was so bad, baiting her like that.

She waved her hand. "He looks trustworthy."

"Then why didn't you tell him everything?"

She blinked as if the answer should be obvious. "Not *that* kind of trustworthy."

I choked back a giggle because I didn't want to offend her. "So, about Tara."

"Look, I didn't withhold that much information." Bobbi Sue flipped the rag up on her shoulder. "All I could get out of Tara was that she was dealing with a situation involving someone she cared about, and she wanted to make sure she had all the facts before she reported anything to law enforcement."

"That's it?"

"Yep."

"Did she act like she was afraid for her life?"

"Maybe." Bobbi Sue squinted. "At the time, I would've described her as burdened—not scared."

"But now?"

"Well, the minute I heard about her *accident*"—she made air quotes—"I knew in my heart someone had killed her."

CHAPTER FIVE

That night, the day's emotion weighed on my chest, and with a yawn, I collapsed in Daddy's recliner. My stomach roared, but I'd already devoured the leftovers from the meals Wanda had brought us when we were in the field. She loved cooking for Grandpa, so I got the benefit of her skills during harvest when she made sure Grandpa, Cory, and I were well fed.

Digging a TV dinner from the depths of my freezer and nuking it had zero appeal.

Maybe after some episodes of *Monk.*

My phone vibrated on the end table and pulled me out of my stupor. It was my stepdad, Dan. For a second, I debated letting it go to voicemail, but since he never called me, my curiosity won. I prayed nothing was wrong with Mom.

"You surviving harvest?" he asked as soon as I answered.

At least this seemed like a social call. "Something like that." I didn't have the energy to spell out the fact that since it had rained, we weren't in the field. He was a nice guy who always tried to relate to my life, but he was a city boy through and through. Mom must've wanted a different experience the second time around.

"Listen, I don't want to meddle, but I just started working with this really nice guy. Your mom and I think he'd be perfect for you, but she told me since it was my idea, I had to ask you."

I didn't feel like unpacking all of the implications in his last statement. Could I trust Dan's judgment? Had Mom ever met the guy? Still, considering the circumstances with Evan and my wish to meet more men, I really needed to keep an open mind. "Send me this guy's dossier, and I'll review it when Grandpa and I are done shelling corn."

Dan chuckled. "Oh, you slay me. His *dossier*."

"Dan, I'm serious. I like to know what I'm dealing with before I agree to a date. At least tell me his name so I can Facebook stalk him." After my last date, I needed to improve my vetting procedures.

"He doesn't do social media. Besides, sometimes you have to let love happen."

"Like you and Mom? Meeting online qualifies as 'letting love happen'? And who doesn't do social media?" What was this dude hiding?

"I'm going to give you grace because you're tired."

Dan was always "giving grace," like he was so superior to the rest of us mortals. "Thanks." I rolled my eyes.

"Tell you what. Since you can't Facebook stalk him, I'll put together a dossier and e-mail it. Get some rest." He paused. "Here's your mom."

"Sweetheart, are you okay?"

"Define *okay*."

She sighed. "Is something else going on that I need to know about?"

I poured out the story of Tara's letter. When I finished, there was silence.

"Mom?"

"I'm here. And I'll be there tomorrow. You need your mom. I should've realized how hard it would be on you, finding that body and all, but with Dan's mother being so sick, we've been going back and forth from the hospital. I'm sorry."

I opened my mouth and snapped it shut before I could ask if Dan would be coming too. It shouldn't matter either way, and Winstons didn't chomp the hand offering to feed us. Literally and figuratively. If Mom was coming, she'd bring food, or at least make it while she was here. "Okay."

"Get some rest, and I'll see you tomorrow. I love you."

"Love you too."

I reached for the remote on my dusty end table and turned on the TV to see what was happening in the world.

"...Tara Fullerton's cause of death has been ruled asphyxiation, and her death is now being investigated as a homicide."

Asphyxiation? Not a broken neck or blunt force trauma?

I put down the chair's footrest, leaned forward, and stared at the handsome anchor who'd already moved onto the next story. My gut had been right all along.

A frisson rolled down my spine. Another killer was roaming around Wildcat Springs. Still, the sick part of me saw the bright side. Detective Perkins most likely had known this information when I'd met with him this morning since he'd already done some investigating.

Maybe he wouldn't see me as a crazy lady after all.

The aroma of bacon pulled me from a fitful sleep. I rolled over and glanced at the clock on my nightstand. 7:14. Yikes. I must've sounded worse than I thought for my mom to be here so early.

Well, it was either my mom or the Pork Fairy, but my mom was a safe bet.

I yanked a sweatshirt over my head and closed my bedroom door on my way out so Mom wouldn't see the pile of clothes in the corner and my unmade bed. I found her flitting around my kitchen. Her honey-colored hair was pulled into a ponytail that, combined with her petite runner's figure, made her look about ten years younger than her actual age.

With a spatula in hand, she rushed around the island and gathered me in a hug. "I'm making scrambled eggs and bacon." She reached up and smoothed my hair.

I yawned and poured coffee. "What time did you get up?"

"Five-thirty-ish. I couldn't sleep anyway." She pointed the spatula toward a file folder sitting on the table. "Dan sent—"

"A dossier." I took a sip of coffee, opened the folder, and examined the stapled papers inside. "He knows I was kidding, right?"

Mom raised her eyebrows. "Were you?"

"Sort of. Kind of. Not really." I skimmed through the bulleted list highlighting Jon Nordmeyer's positive traits. One of Dan's most impressive qualities was his attention to detail, which made him the perfect lawyer to spend his days scrutinizing contracts. The last page had a picture of Jon. Blue eyes. Receding hairline. Nice smile—and teeth.

"What do you think?"

"About?"

"Georgia Rae Winston, drink your coffee and stop being stubborn. You know what I mean."

"Tell Dan this Jon guy looks pretty good—on paper anyway. I'm impressed that he's into triathlons. Is he going to contact me?"

"Only if you give Dan permission."

"I give my consent." I waved the papers around. "Does he need my signature to make it an official contract?"

Mom grinned and turned back toward my stove that—to my surprise—was actually working. "Sweetie, Dan cares about you. It would be nice if you'd be more accepting."

"Wait. Are we seriously having this conversation right now? You know I'm not caffeinated yet." I sat down at the table and buried my head in my arms.

Mom sighed. "Sometimes you make him feel like a second-class citizen."

I raised my head. "If he feels that way, it's his own fault, and he needs to man up. I've been very accepting of him."

And that was the edited version.

"Never mind. Just do me a favor and try harder to be nice. Your version of accepting is different than other people's." She shoved some eggs and bacon onto a plate and slapped it down in front of me. "Eat. Drink your coffee."

"Got it." Try harder to be nice.

That would be a struggle.

The clouds hung low, and a chill hovered in the air, an appropriate dismal atmosphere for Tara Fullerton's funeral.

I slipped inside the Fountain & Son Funeral Home and took a seat on the far-left side in the middle, where I could see the front and back of the crowd. A few people, probably family, sat near the front. Instead of a casket, an urn stood on a table surrounded by pink roses and a picture of Tara.

I caught Detective Perkins's eye, and he nodded. Was he hoping the murderer would show up?

Bobbi Sue gave a subtle wave in my direction, and my cousin J.T. stood in the back. Wait. What was he doing here? Our eyes met, and he shrank against the wall. Before I could get up and go talk to him, the pastor began speaking.

"Tara Rianne Fullerton was born on August 13, 1992, to Deborah Fullerton, who preceded her in death." The pastor continued reading the same obituary that I'd read online. Why did he think this would be a good way to start the service?

Tara—like all of us—was more than a list of vital statistics. She'd laughed. Loved. Cried. Wasn't there a funny story he could've started with? My family'd had plenty of anecdotes to share at Daddy's funeral. If Tara's mom had been alive, surely, she would've protested. I'd never interacted with her much, but I knew she'd adored her daughter.

My throat thickened.

When the pastor was done talking, a man who appeared to be about twenty-five stepped up front, cleared his throat, and ran his hand over his shaved head.

"Hi. I'm Nick—Tara's cousin." His Adam's apple bobbed. "Even though I hate public speaking, I couldn't sit back and not tell people how much Tara meant to me." He shifted and scrolled through his phone. "I had to write down a few notes." He held up the phone, and the crowd chuckled sympathetically.

I stole a glance at Detective Perkins, who was gazing at Nick intently. Would Nick know why Tara had wanted to see me?

"If there was anything that Tara would want you to know, it'd be that she'd changed," Nick said. "About a year ago, Tara started going to church with Mom and me. About a month after that, she told me she'd asked Jesus to forgive her and to fix the mess she'd made of her life."

Tears sprung into my eyes, and I said a silent prayer of thanks that Tara was in Heaven.

"Tara was no angel."

The crowd laughed again, and in the front row, a frail young woman with dishwater-blond hair jerked as if she'd been asleep. She glanced around, and when I met her eyes, she turned away.

"But Jesus made a huge difference in Tara's life," Nick said.

"She was more peaceful—and a lot gentler. She'd want you to know that Jesus can change you, like he changed her." He bowed his head and grasped the bridge of his nose. He took a deep breath and continued with a few entertaining stories.

When he finished, the sleepy woman made her way to the front and clung to the podium. She pushed her hair back from her flushed face. "I'm Morgan Hopewood. Tara's best friend." She closed her eyes for a moment, then opened them and continued. "We've been friends since middle school and even went to culinary school together. She was the most loyal friend I've ever had and—" She pressed a fist to her mouth and scratched her arm as if she could dig out the sorrow. "I'm so sorry. I can't do this." Morgan ducked her head, slinked away, and melted into her seat.

The pastor hurried to the front and gave a short message.

As soon as the service was over, I tried to make a beeline for J.T., but the crowd blocked me, and by the time I made it outside to the sidewalk, his truck was zooming down Pearl Street.

Weird. I'd definitely call him later.

Tara's friends and family streamed out of the brick building while I kept my distance from Detective Perkins, who was also surveying the crowd. I searched for Morgan Hopewood, but she'd disappeared. When I made eye contact with Nick, he strolled over and extended his hand. His grasp was firm, and his gray eyes were kind, but sad.

"Nick Vogler."

"Georgia. You did a great job speaking."

"Thanks. How'd you know Tara?"

"I gave her piano lessons when she was in fifth grade." I glanced at the thinning crowd and lowered my voice. "I was also the one who found her..."

He blinked and loosened his tie. "I'm so sorry."

"No, I'm the one who's sorry. She didn't deserve such an awful fate." I clutched my purse handle.

Nick whipped off the tie and shoved it in his suit pocket. "I keep wracking my brain trying to figure out who would've done this to her."

I said a silent prayer of thanks for the opening. "Any ideas?"

"I can't picture Tara hunting at all, but she recently decided to pick up a new hobby to impress her boyfriend." Nick nodded to his left. "Mike's the guy with the beard and the red flannel shirt."

Flannel. At a funeral.

Mike stood with an older couple, which I pegged as his parents because the man also wore a blue flannel shirt, and Mike had clearly inherited the bump in his nose from the woman. He hadn't been mentioned in the obituary, though I recognized him from Tara's social media posts. "How long had they been dating?"

"A little over a year."

"What's his last name?" I just wanted to make sure I had it right.

"Dunson. I told Tara she should get rid of him because of his criminal record, but she didn't listen." Nick grimaced. "I'll never get over the fact that our last conversation was a fight over her refusing to dump Mike."

"What kind of record?" At that moment, Mike turned and met my eyes. His expression darkened, and he stepped closer.

Nick glanced over my shoulder and lowered his voice. "He got caught hacking some teachers' email accounts when he was a senior in high school. Tara insisted he'd been young and stupid but had changed."

"Did he serve time?"

"No. He paid a fine, and the school expelled him. He wasn't able to graduate."

I bit my lip. I could see why Tara was willing to give him a chance. It wasn't like hacking was a violent crime. "How'd they meet?"

"Tara worked at his restaurant while she was going to culinary school."

"Did Tara ever mention Mike hurting her?" I glanced over Nick's shoulder and saw Detective Perkins edging closer, and Mike had inched within hearing distance. I'd better wrap this up fast.

"No." Nick furrowed his brow. "Are you a detective?"

Detective Perkins raised his eyebrows.

I shifted. "No. I'm just nosy and want to help figure out who did this. Sorry." Just then, a dark-haired woman stepped between the detective and me and asked him a question.

God bless her.

"Don't be. If nosy figures out what happened to Tara, then I'm all for it." Nick fished a silver holder from his pocket and dealt a business card to me. "Call if you have any more questions."

I studied the information as Nick meandered toward Mike and his parents. Nick was the network administrator for the Wells Corporation in Richardville.

Before I could slip away, Detective Perkins caught up with me in the parking lot. "Should I call you Detective Winston?"

His tone indicated he meant it as a joke, but I wasn't in the mood for lightheartedness.

"Nick came over to talk to me. I was just asking a few questions." Mike stared at us, and I turned my back to avoid his smoldering glare.

"Must've been good ones if he thought you were a detective instead of a farmer."

"Farmers can't ask good questions?" I shoved my hands in my coat pockets.

"That's not what I meant."

"Have you talked to Mike Dunson?" I lowered my voice.

49

"Because Tara's cousin seems to think Mike might've killed Tara." Mike's gaze alone was enough to hospitalize someone.

"Please trust us to handle this." Detective Perkins rested his hand on my arm.

I looked him straight in his gorgeous blue eyes and thought of how sincere he'd seemed when he told me he'd look at Daddy's case. The last thing I wanted to do was make him mad and cause him not to prioritize that investigation. Besides, Mike was creeping me out. "Okay. I'll try."

But everything I'd learned wouldn't make it easy.

CHAPTER SIX

When I left the funeral, I decided the best course of action was to talk to J.T.—in person. I wouldn't give him a chance to dodge my phone call. J.T. worked at Wildcat Springs Implement, and part of his responsibilities included selling farm equipment. Though Grandpa and I weren't in need of a combine, tractor, or planter, I *was* in the market for a new lawn mower, so I drove to the dealership that was located outside of Wildcat Springs in the middle of a field.

J.T.'d get me a good deal and give me some answers as to why he was at Tara's funeral. I entered the showroom, and the smell of motor oil mingled with popcorn lingered in the air. Several models of lawnmowers were displayed in the large showroom, and a row of offices lined the wall on the left. J.T. sat in the office behind the third window, and he was talking on the phone.

"Hey, Georgia!" Max Jenkins, the owner and former Wildcat Springs High School football legend, ambled out of his office. "What can I do for you?" He jingled the change in his pocket and flashed a toothy grin.

I pointed to a zero-turn mower. "I could use a new mower

and thought you might have some good end-of-the season deals." My farmhouse, barns, and grain bins sat on five acres, and mowing the lawn took up a lot of time, so I figured I should have equipment that made it enjoyable.

"We'll fix you right up." Max glanced over his shoulder. "I'll send J.T. out when he's done, since you like to work with him." He turned to get J.T. and then stopped. "Say, how's your mom?"

"She and Dan are doing great."

"Glad to hear it." Max had taken my mom on a few dates after Daddy died, but the relationship hadn't blossomed. "I've been seeing someone new, and it's going well."

"Good for you." I tried not to appear too interested.

Max pointed to the popcorn machine in the corner. "Help yourself while you're waiting."

"Thanks." Since I hadn't eaten lunch, I filled a red and white striped bag and started munching while I studied the photos of the old tractors hanging on the walls. I was sure glad I was farming in the modern era with my air-conditioned cabs and autosteer.

"I had a feeling I'd see you today."

I whirled around and faced J.T. "That's funny. I don't remember mentioning I need a new mower."

He crossed his arms. "Do you need a mower, or are you here to find out why I was at Tara's funeral?"

He knew me well. "Both." I tossed more popcorn in my mouth.

"Which one were you looking at?"

I swallowed. "Zero turn."

"Come on back, and I'll get you some information."

We entered his office, and he motioned toward the chair in front of his desk. "Can I get you something to drink? We have Coke products and water."

52

"A Coke would be great." Someone had gotten carried away when putting butter and salt on the popcorn.

He handed me a few lawn mower brochures from the display rack on the wall. "Take a look at these, and I'll be right back."

Even though I was a customer, J.T. was family, and he was being strangely formal. So he knew Tara well enough to go to her funeral. Lots of people did.

"Here you go." He thrust the Coke can at me and closed the door.

I cracked the can open. "Why are you being weird?"

"Why are you being nosy?" He narrowed his eyes.

"I had no idea you and Tara were friends." I sipped the Coke.

"Well, we were. Back in high school." He leaned against his desk, picked up a toy tractor on his desk, and spun a wheel. "She was in the color guard when I was in marching band." He put the tractor back, walked around his desk, and sat. "I haven't always had the best luck with girls, and Tara made me feel special."

I understood having bad luck with the opposite sex. "I'm sorry you lost a friend." Had they been more than friends? I wanted to ask so badly but remembered Life Lesson #27: Always mind your own business. I wasn't so good at adhering to that precept. Still, J.T.'s behavior made the answer obvious, which staved off the temptation to nose around.

"Thanks." He stared out the window at the row of tractors lined up in the lot next to the building. "Tara always knew how to make me laugh."

"That's a great quality." If I couldn't laugh with Brandi and Ashley, I'd go crazy, though they'd probably say that my antics entertained them more than anything they ever did to amuse me. "Were you in contact with Tara recently?"

"No. We hadn't talked in several years." He tugged at the collar on his gray polo shirt, which had the Wildcat Spring Implement logo embroidered on it. "Why?"

I told him about the letter and what I'd learned from Bobbi Sue.

"Wow." J.T. blew out a breath and rested his head in his hands, his man bun bobbing slightly.

How did Max feel about J.T.'s new hairstyle? Did he worry about it being a turn off to the more conservative customers? Maybe not since J.T. was a great salesman—second only to Max. J.T.'d even earned a cruise last year.

The silence jumped into awkward territory, and I fidgeted with the fringe that lined the hem of my sweater. J.T. had always been sensitive, so I should probably back off. "I can come back another day."

He snapped his head up. "Nope. I'm fine." He turned his chair toward the computer. "Let's see what kind of deal I can get you on that mower."

Wednesday afternoon, I worked in my office, trying to catch up managing our farm budget since the fields were too wet to shell corn. Instead of accounting, I kept thinking about Tara Fullerton and the family and friends she'd left behind. I knew what it felt like to have unanswered questions.

Finding Tara's body and receiving the note involved me—whether I liked it or not. I tapped my pen against the desk and tried to remember my vow to stay away because letting Detective Perkins handle everything was the wisest choice.

Besides, I hadn't been able to figure out what had happened to Daddy. What made me think I could help with Tara's case?

I considered the facts I'd already learned about Tara. Maybe there was a small lead I could follow up on. Speak with one of Tara's friends. Her friend Morgan Hopewood would be a good person to talk to, but her behavior at the funeral disturbed me.

Wait a second.

I turned to my computer and typed the words *symptoms of opioid high* into a search engine because, unfortunately, opioid abuse was becoming more and more prevalent. Last year the number of overdose deaths in Richard County had doubled.

I surveyed the results. Flushed, itchy skin, sleepiness, fixed pupils. Morgan hit several indicators, though I hadn't gotten close enough to see her pupils.

Did she have an addiction problem, or had she overmedicated to deal with the pain of losing a friend?

I drummed my finger against my desk and thought of a different option. Tara had posted on social media about working out at Fitness Universe in Richardville, and the gym wasn't that far away. Before I could change my mind, I hurried to get my shoes and keys.

When I arrived twenty minutes later, Fitness Universe's parking lot only had a few cars, which wasn't surprising since it was the middle of the afternoon. I put up the hood on my sweatshirt and sprinted through the rain. At the front desk, a middle-aged woman waited with a companion—her cleavage.

"May I help you?"

I smiled. "Did you know Tara Fullerton?"

"Yes." The woman's eyes clouded. "You with the police?"

"No. I'm doing a private investigation into her death." That was a stretch, but I wasn't sure what else to say.

"You a real PI?"

"N—"

"I've always wanted to meet a PI. Do you go on lots of stakeouts?"

"I—"

"Have you ever caught a man cheating on his wife? I thought about hiring a PI when I thought my husband was having an affair. I used the money for a boob job instead."

I choked back a laugh. "Did it work?"

She frowned and pointed to her friends. "The boob job? Sure it did. I hired a good surgeon."

"I mean—"

"Oh, right. Did I hang onto my husband?" She beamed, glanced down at her chest, and shimmied her shoulders. "Did the trick."

I cleared my throat. "I'm glad. Now, about Tara."

"Real shame." The woman shook her head. "I'm Susan, by the way."

"Georgia."

She nodded. "Tara used to come here almost every day. She was a sweetheart. I can't think of why anyone would've wanted to kill her."

"Are any of her friends here now?"

"Let me check." She leaned over, and her nails clicked against the keyboard. "Kevin Doyle's here. He's one tough guy. Spent several years in the army disposing of explosives." She shook her head as she turned the monitor so I could see his profile picture.

Kevin had been at the funeral.

"He's probably lifting," Susan said. "Go on in. Normally, we don't admit non-members, but since you're an investigator..."

"Thank you, Susan."

I pushed through the door into the exercise area and wrinkled my nose at the odor of sweat and rubber. It was also about fifteen degrees colder. Threading my way through treadmills and weight machines, I zeroed in on Kevin, who was bench pressing with a spotter. I hovered next to a leg curl machine until he finished with a grunt.

"Kevin Doyle?"

"Yeah?" Irritation filled his tone, and the tattooed man he was working with gave me the once over. Kevin sat up, and his face changed when he saw me. "Can I help you?" He ran his fingers through his brown hair.

"I'm investigating Tara Fullerton's death."

He sighed, picked up a towel, and mopped his forehead. I tried not to stare at his left hand, which was missing his pinky and ring fingers.

"I can't believe she's gone." He stood and walked closer, and his spotter wandered away. Kevin nodded toward the man. "He didn't know Tara. Just started working out here."

"Did she have any enemies?"

He scoffed and draped the towel around his neck. "Tara? Nah. She was tough, but she hid it behind a sweet exterior—most of the time."

"How long did you know her?"

"A while."

"Did you know her friend Morgan?"

He nodded. "Sort of. She worked out a time or two with Tara."

"Does Morgan have a drug addiction?"

"Honestly, I don't know, but I get why you're asking—'cause she sure seemed strung out at Tara's funeral, didn't she?"

"Yeah." I decided I'd better move on before he got impatient. "Hey, where did Tara work? Her family didn't mention it in the obituary."

He looked above my head as if the rafters could supply the answer. "Some cooking school called Eatable."

I stored that detail. "There's something else I'm curious about. How long had Tara been hunting?"

"Like ten seconds?" He snorted. "She took it up to impress that boyfriend of hers, and I don't know why because I can't picture her bagging a deer. She loved animals. In fact, she hit a squirrel a couple of weeks ago on the way here, and I thought we were going to have to get her a tranquilizer."

"Really?" I thought of my own overreaction to hitting a rabbit the day I'd found Tara's body. Had she been upset about something else and killing the animal had magnified her reaction?

"Okay, okay, my friends know I exaggerate." He held up a hand. "It wasn't *that* bad, but she was upset, for sure."

"Did you ever meet her boyfriend?"

"Yeah." Kevin scrunched up his face. "Seemed like a nice enough guy. I only met him the one time he came here with her." He leaned forward. "Truth be told, I practically bit my tongue into hamburger to keep from telling Mike that Tara was two-timing him."

My eyes widened. "Seriously? Did you know who she was seeing?"

He shook his head. "Some dude in Wildcat Springs she called *Sharkie*."

J.T.'s reaction to Tara's death came to mind, but I brushed the thought away. He'd never date a girl who had a boyfriend. Unless he hadn't known. I thumbed my birthstone ring. "How long had Tara been seeing this Sharkie guy?"

"A month or two."

Surely J.T. hadn't lied to me. "Thanks. You've been helpful."

"Cool. You got a card or anything in case I remember something else?" He clutched each end of the towel and shifted casually.

"Sure." I dug through my purse, withdrew a business card, and handed it to him.

"Winston Family Farms?" He frowned. "I thought you said you were an investigator."

"I wear a lot of hats." I got out of the gym and back to my truck as fast as I could.

As soon as I was back in my truck, I searched on my phone for Eatable and found it was on the south side of Richardville. Definitely worth the short trip. I pulled into traffic and drove across town.

Eatable was located in a strip mall between a nail salon and a Chinese restaurant. As I walked in, the bell jingled. In front of me was a gigantic home ec room. Six separate kitchens with stainless steel appliances lined the walls to my right and left. A large common area stood in the middle with chairs and a demonstration station trimmed in weathered, reclaimed wood. The pale green walls gave the room a soothing, homey feeling.

A middle-aged woman in a white coat and checkered pants emerged from a door in the back wall. Everything about her—body, cheeks, and glasses—was round. "Welcome to Eatable. Are you here for the five o'clock class?"

"No. I—"

"Perhaps I can interest you in one of our three levels of culinary workshops." She reached for a stack of fliers sitting on a table by the door and handed me the paper with class descriptions and times. "Our goal is to help you make your food *eatable*." She giggled.

I'd certainly stumbled into the right place. "I could use some classes, but that's not why I came today."

She tilted her head and furrowed her brow. "How can I help you then?" A bit of iciness crept into her tone.

"I'm investigating the death of Tara Fullerton."

"Oh!" Tears sprang into the woman's eyes. "She was *such* a dear girl. Her mother and I were friends for years before she died. I hired Tara to teach some of our advanced classes since she'd been to culinary school. Our clients *loved* her." She held out her hand. "I'm Pam Marconi, by the way."

"Georgia Winston." I grasped her hand. "So she hadn't made anyone mad?"

"Oh no. I give our clients a survey at the end of each class, and Tara *always* received high marks."

"What about her relationship with the other employees?"

"I *never* heard any complaints about her, but then sometimes employees don't speak freely in front of the boss. If you get a chance, talk to Morgan Hopewood to see if she has any ideas. She was Tara's best friend, but she's on vacation."

Or her vacation was actually rehab. "Does Morgan have a drug problem? She seemed a little strung out at Tara's funeral."

Pam knitted her brows. "Not to my knowledge. She was probably just grieving. When my husband died five years ago, I *had* to pop pills to make it through his funeral. I can barely remember that day." She stepped closer and lowered her voice, even though we were alone. "If I were you, I'd take a look Tara's former boss, Mike Dunson. Not long ago, when I called him for a reference, one of the employees put the phone down to go get him, and I could hear him ripping somebody up one side and down the other. I can't imagine treating an employee that way. I'd *never* sleep at night."

Clearly, she didn't realize Mike had also been Tara's boyfriend. "Did Tara ever mention a friend named Sharkie?"

"Not that I recall."

The bell on the door jingled, and a hipster and his matching female companion entered.

"Welcome," Pam said. "Are you here for our five o'clock class?"

"Yes. We're a little early." Hipster motioned toward the young woman. "This is my girlfriend Destiny. I'm Travis —Cooper."

"Nice to meet you both." Pam pointed to the demonstration area. "Please have a seat. I'll be with you in a moment." She turned back to me. "I'm sorry, but we need to wrap this up."

"One more question. Did Tara ever talk about hunting?"

Pam tilted her head and furrowed her brow. "No. I was *flab-bergasted* when I heard she died while hunting."

Interesting. "Thanks for your help."

"You're welcome." She motioned toward the flier in my hand. "Please come back and take a class. It makes a *wonderful* date night."

I was sure it did. I'd just have to have a date first.

CHAPTER SEVEN

A fter I left Eatable, I decided to take Pam Marconi's advice and talk to Mike Dunson, who owned a restaurant in downtown Richardville. I hoped that even though he'd creeped me out at Tara's funeral, he might lighten up if I bought supper at his place. In spite of the day's chaos, my stomach roared.

I found a public parking lot and hoofed it across the street to the old train station that housed Mike's Sandwich Depot. A handful of customers sat at wooden booths that lined the exposed brick walls. The lack of people made me wonder about the quality of the food.

A sign indicated I should be seated, so I found a booth in the back. A pretty server, with full cheeks that probably made her look younger than she was, stood up from a table where she was studying, sauntered over, and handed me a menu. A blue and purple butterfly tattoo partially disguised a scar on her wrist.

"I'm Haley. I'll be taking care of you today. Ham and cheese Stromboli's on special."

"That sounds perfect, and I'll have a Coke too."

She withdrew a pad from her apron and scribbled my order. "Okie-dokie."

I returned the menu. "Is Mike here?"

"Yeah. Why?" She flipped her ponytail over her shoulder.

"May I talk to him?"

She jabbed her order pad back into her apron. "I'll let him know."

After Haley brought my Coke and informed me that Mike would be out soon, she returned to her table and buried her head in a book. Never a good sign when a waitress had time to study during her shift. I took a crayon from the Mason jar on the table and doodled flowers on the butcher paper.

"Haley said you wanted to see me." Mike loomed over my table. He wore a green flannel shirt and an apron splattered with tomato sauce—at least I hoped it was tomato sauce.

"Georgia Winston." I stuck out my hand.

"You was at Tara's funeral." His eyes narrowed.

"Yes, sir. If you don't mind, I have a few questions about Tara."

"Why?" He scowled and set his jaw.

Since the last thing I wanted was for him to realize I considered him a suspect, I picked the reason I hoped would put him at ease. "Tara contacted me before she died because she needed my help with a situation in her life. We never got a chance to meet, so I feel some responsibility to try to help find her killer. I thought you might be able to point me in the right direction."

Mike relaxed his expression. "Don't know that I got the answers. Found out last Thursday that she was seein' another guy behind my back. So what do I know?" He crossed his hairy arms. "But go ahead."

I met his eyes and dropped the crayon back in the jar. "Who told you Tara was cheating?"

63

"Her little friend Morgan." Mike screwed up his face. "I didn't believe her, because she didn't have any proof. Not sure why she felt the need to tell me after Tara was gone. Besides, Morgan is trouble. Tried to bilk money out of Tara so she could fund her drug habit." He waved a finger at me. "I told Tara not to waste her time on that piece of trash, but she didn't listen. Thought she could help."

Yikes. "Did Tara give her money?"

"Nope. According to Tara, they had a cat fight over it." He chuckled. "I'd have paid a week's profit to witness that."

Ugh. In spite of the fact this guy was a jerk, I had to keep him talking. "Were you upset when Tara left here to work at Eatable?"

"Nope." Mike's face softened as he sat across from me in the booth. "I was proud of her. She'd worked hard in culinary school and had a bigger future ahead of her than working here the rest of her life. She had talent that could've led to her own cooking show. That's why she wanted to teach people—it was good practice."

I switched gears. "How long had Tara been interested in hunting?"

He stroked his beard. "About a month before deer season, she came to me and said she wanted to learn. I was blown away. Here was a girl who freaked out about hitting a squirrel with her car."

That lined up with what Kevin Doyle at Fitness Universe had said.

"Still, I took it as a peace offering since we'd hit a rough patch, so I taught her how to use a crossbow. Helped her with target practice. I even promised to take her out to my favorite hunting spot once the season opened." Mike's pain-filled eyes met mine. "But she had an excuse when I asked her to go on opening day. Now I wonder if she went with her new guy."

I wondered that too. "Did she ever say she thought she was in danger?"

Haley arrived with my Stromboli.

"Thanks." I unrolled my silverware.

"You're welcome." She nodded and scurried away. I made a mental note to ask her about Mike before I left.

"Nope." Mike put his elbows on the table and rested his head in his hands. "If she was, she probably confided in her new boyfriend." He stood. "We done here? I got work to do, and you need to eat while it's hot."

I shook my head and held up a finger while I dug a business card from my handbag and handed it to Mike. "Call me if you think of anything else."

"Will do." He trudged back to the kitchen.

When I finished eating the Stromboli, that was actually really good, Haley brought me my check. "Do you need a refill in a to-go cup?"

"No thanks."

"You can pay up front. Have a nice evening." She smiled and turned.

"Wait."

"Yes?" She faced me and stuffed her hands in her apron pocket.

"How is it, working for Mike?"

"Fine. The pay's decent." She motioned toward her stack of schoolbooks. "I'm in college, and he lets me study when we're not busy." She stepped closer and lowered her voice. "He's been a total grump lately, but I figure it's because he's torn up about his girlfriend dying. Anyway, I've got to get back to studying for my organic chemistry test tomorrow, so have a nice evening."

Grandpa, Cory, and I spent Thursday, Friday, and part of Saturday shelling corn, which gave me plenty of time in the combine cab to ponder everything I'd learned about Tara.

Eventually, I'd come to the conclusion that finding answers wasn't worth alienating Detective Perkins and forced the subject out of my mind. Not only did I want the detective to ask me on a date, but I also needed him to give Daddy's case his best effort. Besides, the only real benefit of my little investigation was that it'd taken my focus off of Evan and Baby Kelsey.

When a storm rolled in Saturday afternoon, and the field got wet enough that we had to stop, I took a nap before heading to Brandi's house that night for dessert and a *Psych* marathon.

After we made sundaes, I brought Brandi and Ashley up to speed on my stepdad meddling in my love life because in comparison to the investigation, Detective Perkins, and Evan, it was a safe, but juicy, topic. Even though I'd rehearsed all of Jon Nordmeyer's great qualities, Detective Perkins's face lingered in my mind. I did my best to push him right back out.

I put my empty bowl on the coffee table and leaned back on the couch.

"Your stepdad might be on to something with Jon." Brandi was tucking away chocolate chip ice cream while her Yorkie perched next to her on the loveseat.

"I agree." Ashley held up her spoon in an affirmative vote. "Put yourself out there and give him a chance."

"Fine." I crossed my arms. If I told them my reluctance was a self-defense mechanism designed to protect me from false hope, they'd tell me to see a counselor or get a dog.

Again.

Brandi shook her head and grinned. "You met a former student of mine earlier this week at Fitness Universe."

Uh-oh. "Who's that?" I donned my best innocent expression.

"Kevin Doyle." She licked her spoon and put her bowl on the

coffee table next to mine. "He was in my U.S. History class when I taught at Richardville." She picked up Gigi and stroked her head.

"What'd he say about me?"

Ashley leaned forward. "Is he good looking? Single? Nice?" She turned to Brandi. "If he doesn't want to go out with Georgia, would he consider me?"

I stared at Ashley. "Easy there, killer."

Brandi chuckled and shrugged. "I don't know. That's not why I brought him up, though."

"Okay." Ashley huffed and stirred her chocolate ice cream. "Then why?"

"I ran into Kevin at the drugstore today, and he said he met this girl from Wildcat Springs. Wondered if I knew a *PI* named Georgia."

"Well, you don't." I pulled my sweatshirt sleeves over my hands. "You know a farmer named Georgia."

The edge of Brandi's mouth twitched, and her eyes danced. "Care to explain?"

She knew me well enough to realize with Georgia Rae Winston anything was possible—including a second or third career. "No wonder you wanted us to come over for ice cream. You had to get the *scoop*." I fought a snort of laughter over my own stupid pun.

Brandi and Ashley groaned in unison.

"You caught me," Brandi said. "Now out with it, already."

I pulled a pillow into my lap and propped my bare feet up on the coffee table. "I went to the gym where Tara Fullerton worked out." I told them about my visit with Kevin and how I'd gone to Eatable and Mike's Sandwich Depot.

Ashley giggled. "Good work, detective."

"Georgia Rae, the sheriff's department can handle death investigations," Brandi said in her teacher voice. "You're interfering. TV detectives don't like it, so I doubt the real ones do either." She gave me the ultimate mom glare, and I swore even Gigi frowned at me.

I traced my fingers over the pillow's floral pattern. It was so wrong that Brandi didn't have children to mother, because she'd be awfully good at it. "You're right. But I got to thinking about Tara's family and how they feel—losing her and all..." My throat tightened. "Besides, think how you'd feel if one of your former students wrote you a letter asking for help. Wouldn't you want to find out why?"

"I would." Ashley reached over and put her arm around me. "I totally get it."

"I've decided to back off. When I took Detective Perkins that letter Tara sent me, he told me he's looking into my daddy's case. The last thing I want to do is make him mad. I need him to give Daddy's case his best effort."

"Are you sure that's the *only* reason you don't want the detective mad at you?" Ashley eyed me.

Heat crept up my neck. "What other reason would there be?"

"Hot and single come to mind." She smirked.

"How'd you find that out?"

"I overheard him questioning Bobbi Sue at Latte Conspiracies the other day. I tried to get him to look my way, but he was a man on a mission." Ashley stuck her lip out.

"Can we talk about something else?" Anything. Calculus. Engineering. Softball. U.S. History.

"Absolutely." Brandi picked up the empty bowls and walked toward the kitchen as Gigi trotted behind. She paused and looked over her shoulder. "How about we take bets on how long it is before Jon calls and asks you out?"

"No." I rolled my eyes. "Winstons don't gamble."

Winstons also never farmed on Sunday. Ever. Well, except the year when Grandpa and Daddy had been behind on harvesting because the weather had been awful. One November Sunday after church, Grandpa shelled corn while Daddy drove the tractor with the auger cart.

And the combine caught on fire.

They both considered it a sign of God's wrath, and since I'd grown up hearing that story, this truth had been pounded into my very being. Besides, I figured I was in enough trouble with God because of my swearing problem that I didn't need to add breaking the Sabbath to my naughty list.

Because Sunday farming was off the table, I found myself on the hook for hosting my Bible study group on a beautiful, dry evening, and I couldn't use harvest as an excuse, though Grandpa and I would shell corn on Monday.

I stood in my kitchen staring at the stack of pizza boxes that I'd gone into Wildcat Springs to pick up because, of course, Pizza Heaven didn't deliver all the way out to my farm. But they should. I'd probably increase their business by ten percent.

I'd meant to buy pies for dessert—our group loved them—but Pastry Delight was closed, and Hometown Market was out by the time I'd remembered. They'd have to make do with the ice cream bars I'd purchased instead.

Glancing at the clock, I sighed. Ten minutes until I had to slap on my happy hostess face—even though everyone in the group knew that I did *not* have the spiritual gift of hospitality— and Evan would be showing up with Baby Kelsey in tow.

I'd caught a glimpse of them across the church earlier that day as she'd clung to his arm during worship time.

The front door creaked. "Come in!" I started pulling two-liter bottles of pop from the fridge and sticking them on the counter.

The night before, I'd given Brandi and Ashley strict instructions that they were to show up ten minutes early, so I wouldn't have to be alone with Evan and Kelsey.

"Hey, Georgia."

Evan.

I will not cuss on Sunday... I will not cuss on Sunday.

I closed the refrigerator door and rushed forward. "Evan." I forced a smile. "And you must be Kelsey. It's so nice to meet you. I've heard so many nice things about you." My words sounded robotic.

Her mouth stretched into a tight-lipped smile, and she looked me up and down. "That's good." She shoved her hands in the pockets of her green, military-inspired jacket.

The girl had good taste.

I retreated to the freezer to retrieve some ice and wished I could shut myself inside and ponder how I'd ever thought Evan could be attracted to me, because she was different from me in every physical way possible.

Young. Chin-length black hair. Olive skin. Blue eyes. Petite build. Thin.

No wonder he didn't want me. I was too old, too blond, too brown-eyed, too pale, too tall, and too curvy. Pretty? Sure, why not? Exotic?

Not even close.

"Would you like something to drink?" I shut the freezer door a little too vigorously.

Kelsey eyed the pop bottles, and her nose wrinkled. "I don't do pop. Not even diet. Do you have sparkling water?"

As far as I was concerned, no one could do pop, do church, or do life but that was a totally different issue, and I didn't have time to ponder the painful death of the English language when I was dying one of my own. "I have well water."

Evan frowned. "Do you have bottled water? Your water can be a little, um—"

"No. Sorry." I cringed. Why hadn't I picked up a case of water?

"I've got a bottle that I haven't opened." Brandi breezed in and thrust the bottle at Kelsey, who blinked a few times but took it.

Thank you God for Brandi and her hatred of my well water.

"Thanks," Evan said. "You're a lifesaver."

Lifesaver? How about a slice of pepperoni with a side of drama?

"Yeah, thanks," Kelsey said, and her gaze fell on the stack of pizza boxes.

"I hope pizza's okay." I yanked open the refrigerator and buried my head inside. "If not, I have some lettuce. I could whip up a salad." I pulled a lone carrot from the vegetable drawer, faced them, and waved the withered vegetable around. "It's your lucky day because I have more than lettuce. Low-fat ranch dressing too. You've hit the jackpot. I'm not exactly *Top Chef* material." I emitted a laugh that ended with a choke.

Evan and Brandi stared at me.

"Pizza's fine." Kelsey moved closer to Evan, who wrapped a protective arm around her.

"Don't worry. I ordered cheese. I always do. Sometimes sausage makes my stomach hurt. I've never been able to figure out why. I'm okay if I drink milk, though."

Brandi moved between Kelsey and me. "Tell me about your nursing job."

Relief flooded Kelsey's expression, and she started talking about working with cancer patients as Brandi led her to the living room. I took refuge in the walk-in pantry and searched for the paper plates I'd forgotten to put out.

When I turned around with a stack of plates clutched to my chest, Evan was blocking the door.

"Are you okay?" he asked.

"Yep."

"You're lying."

"And now you're a mind reader? Wherever did that talent come from, and why have you kept it hidden for so long? It must be great when you're able to get inside the heads of teenagers. Is it scary inside their minds? Never mind. I don't want to know."

He put his hand on the doorframe and displayed his bicep. "You were lying to me the other day in the combine cab too, weren't you?"

"Of course not." I studied the flower pattern on the plates and ran my finger along the edge of the stack. "I don't want to scare Kelsey off. She's important to you, and I'm trying to be hospitable when we all know I'm not."

He grinned. Oh, why did he have to look so handsome?

"That's what I appreciate about you, Georgia. But, relax." He rested his hand on my arm, and I said a silent prayer of thanks my sweater covered the goosebumps rising under my sleeve. "What Kelsey and I have is rock solid. You can't scare her away."

Really? Rock solid after a few weeks? I ignored my twisting gut and nodded. "Good for you. I've had other things on my mind." I lowered my voice. "I was looking into Tara Fullerton's case." Why was I telling Evan when a much better choice would've been, well, pretty much *anyone*?

He raised his eyebrows. "Why not let the police handle it?"

"Tara sent me a letter before she died because she wanted to meet with me, so I poked around a little—but I've backed off."

He drew in a sharp breath. "Wow. That's crazy." Evan stepped out of the doorway and motioned for me to go ahead. "I'm not surprised you were looking into things."

"Why?" I stopped and faced him.

"Everyone knows the only person you trust is yourself." He laughed, and I curled my fingers into a fist. "Just kidding." He gave me a friendly punch on the arm.

But we both knew he wasn't.

After everyone in my Bible study group had gone home, I gathered greasy pizza boxes and hefted a full trash bag out of the wastebasket in my kitchen. Evan's words still rankled. How dare he judge me after everything I'd been through? It wasn't like he didn't know about my dad's murder. Stomping to the garage, I deposited the trash into the large bin and banged the lid. How could he come into my home and mock me with his "rock solid" relationship?

I slammed the back door as my phone started ringing. When I picked it up from the kitchen table, I didn't recognize the number. Was it Jon sent to distract me from Evil Evan and Baby Kelsey? I decided to answer.

"Georgia, this is Jon Nordmeyer."

I blinked. I never had that kind of luck, which was mainly why I never gambled. "Hey. How's it going?" I walked into my living room and spotted Kelsey's jacket draped over my piano bench. Lucky for her, it wouldn't fit me.

"Great. Your stepdad gave me your number. I hope it's okay that I called."

"Absolutely." After all, I *had* approved the dossier. Dan moved fast, but then, I already knew that. He'd wooed my mom in less than six months. I paced in front of the fireplace, and as I opened my mouth to fill the silence with some Georgia-esque babbling, Jon cleared his throat.

"Look, I'd like to meet in person—wasting time talking about frou-frou stuff over email and phone calls is annoying. By the time I meet you, I'll never remember what your favorite color or band is."

I stopped and used my thumb to brush dust off Daddy's

photo on the mantle. Ten points for Jon's honesty. Dan knew more about me than I'd given him credit for. "Red. Chanticleer— I prefer choral music to bands. I give a pop quiz on the first date. A perfect score means you move on to the next level." I slapped my hand against my forehead and squeezed my eyes shut. I had *not* intended for that to sound suggestive.

At all.

"I have two tickets to see *Wicked* in Indianapolis. Do you want to come?"

I stifled a squeal. I'd been dying to see that musical. "Yes, please." I also said a silent prayer of thanks that my unintended innuendo had flown over his head.

"Excellent. Will Friday work?"

As soon as I ended my conversation with Jon, Evan texted about Kelsey's jacket. He was on his way to pick it up.

Because, of course, it was too scary for her to get it herself.

He didn't say that, but I drew my own conclusions.

When the doorbell chimed, I opened the door and thrust the jacket at Evan. "Here you go."

"Thanks. Kelsey's always leaving stuff everywhere." He chuckled. "It's her one flaw."

It took a valiant effort to turn my burgeoning snort into a passable throat clear, but I somehow managed. "She seems nice."

"She liked everyone in our group—including you." He leaned against the doorframe.

"Really?"

"Yeah, she's just shy until you get to know her, but she told me on the way home that she has a coworker who'd be perfect for you. Maybe we could even double date sometime."

If I'd ever doubted that God worked in all things for good, I'd have become a believer that very moment, because I'd never been so thankful for my meddling stepdad. I shifted. "Actually, I have a date this weekend, but if things don't work out..."

"Great. Let us know." He beamed. "Have a great week." He turned and jogged down the sidewalk.

"You too." I locked the door, leaned against it, and closed my eyes.

Jon Nordmeyer had better be everything Dan had promised.

On a sunny Monday afternoon, Grandpa and I were back shelling corn with Cory's help. J.T. was even planning to assist when he was done with work.

The corn combine header had always reminded me of a giant's comb, and as it crumpled the dry stalks, the sound of crinkling paper blended with the hum of machinery. Bright yellow ears mingled with torn leaves and stalks. While I made a pass down the field, I thought about my upcoming date with Jon.

Even though this week would be full of work, I wasn't second-guessing my decision to go with Jon for a few hours on Friday night.

My mind drifted to Detective Perkins, but I didn't let my thoughts linger there and turned them to his great aunt. I needed to pay a visit to Beverly to make sure she was okay since she hadn't been at church on Sunday.

I glanced at the yield monitor. *Fabulous.* Why had it gone black? *Add that to the list of things going wrong.* I tapped the screen and tried to make adjustments, but the monitor stayed frozen. I stopped the combine because this problem needed my full attention.

I searched my phone for J.T.'s number. Not only did he sell equipment, he was my go-to guy at Wildcat Springs Implement because he knew how to fix technology problems. When I glanced up, crimson words in a dripping-blood font appeared on the yield monitor.

I dropped my phone in my lap and sucked in a breath.

Georgia—Stop poking your nose where it doesn't belong, or you'll be the next to die.

CHAPTER EIGHT

I stopped the combine and stared at the monitor. Shaking my head, I picked up my phone and took several pictures in case the message disappeared. As creepy as the threat was, I couldn't help but worry we might've lost valuable data from this year's harvest.

I called Grandpa.

"What's going on over there?" he asked.

"Someone hacked our yield monitor."

Grandpa chuckled. "Well, if that don't beat all. I knew these technological developments would cause problems. Did we lose data?"

"I'm not sure, but there's a more pressing issue at the moment." I repeated the message.

He muttered something that I couldn't make out. "I'm calling the sheriff's department."

"Ask for Detective Perkins."

Because he was investigating Tara's case. That was the only reason.

While Grandpa made that call, I scrolled through my phone's

contacts and selected J.T.'s number because I'd need his help if I couldn't get the monitor back to normal. "Hey, cuz," I said after his voice message beeped. "I'm shelling corn in our field over on 1000 East, and my yield monitor got hacked, so Grandpa and I are a little worried about data loss. If you can come to my rescue, that'd be great." I disconnected and opened a bottle of water and stared at the message that continued to scroll across the screen. It would take someone tech savvy to pull this off. Clearly, my nosiness had spooked someone into taking action.

Obviously, I was better at this investigation thing than I'd thought.

I sipped my water and considered possible suspects.

Mike Dunson had a history of hacking, and if he'd killed Tara, of course he'd want me to stay away. Goosebumps erupted on my arms as I remembered his threatening gaze at Tara's funeral. Not to mention Tara's cousin had suspected him as well, but Mike had shown his softer side when I'd spoken to him at his restaurant.

Nick Vogler was a network administrator. He might have the expertise to hack the monitor, but why would he have killed his cousin? Perhaps he was the one with a secret, and Tara had intended to investigate Nick. Could her investigation have exposed something he wanted to stay hidden?

Grandpa climbed up the ladder. I scooted over to the instructional seat so he could check out the monitor.

"You'd better be minding your own business." He adjusted his baseball cap.

"I know." The seriousness of the situation was beginning to get through my thick skull.

As Detective Perkins parked on the edge of the field and picked his way across broken cornstalks, the monitor's screen returned to normal and displayed a map of our field with green, yellow, orange, and red patches, indicating the number of bushels we'd harvested. Grandpa and I got out of the cab to greet him, and he grinned when he saw me. "Causing trouble, Miss Winston?"

I shot him a glare and held out my phone. "I didn't do this on purpose."

"Relax. I'm just giving you a hard time." His dimple faded as he studied the picture of the threat. "I'll definitely check this out." He handed my phone back, squinted, and held his hand up to shade his eyes. "Besides talking to Nick Vogler at Tara's funeral, have you done anything else that would constitute poking around?"

I burrowed the toe of my work boot into some smashed cornstalks. Might as well come clean. "I went to Tara's gym to ask questions, and I visited her workplace and spoke with her boss. I also went to see Mike Dunson at his restaurant." I held up my hands in surrender. "But I promise I backed off after that. We've been in the field."

"Why in the Sam Hill would you do that, Georgia Rae?" Grandpa lifted his baseball cap off his head and set it back down.

"It's complicated."

"No. It's simple. You let these guys do their jobs. They're the ones qualified. Not you."

"I have to agree with your grandpa," Detective Perkins said.

Even though it was sunny, the air was crisp, so I zipped my fleece and squirmed under the detective's intense gaze. "Do you think Mike Dunson could've hacked my yield monitor?" I rubbed my arms.

Detective Perkins pressed his lips together. "I'll look into it."

"Is he a suspect?" I tugged my braid when Grandpa shot me a puzzled glance.

"No comment."

"Is there more evidence than the note?"

"There are some text messages on Tara's phone that caught

our attention." Detective Perkins rested his hand on my shoulder. "Relax. I've got this."

"That's right," Grandpa said. "You've got enough to worry about with harvest."

A Ford truck pulled into the grass alongside the road, and J.T. hopped out and joined us. Detective Perkins surveyed J.T., and his eyes lingered for a second on his man bun. Then Detective Perkins held out his hand. "Detective Calvin Perkins."

"J.T. Simms." He grasped the detective's hand. "Georgia, never in my time of working with yield monitors have I ever heard of one being hacked."

"Well, I *am* one-of-a-kind."

"I know. God broke the mold after he made you." J.T.'s eyes twinkled, but when I held out my phone so he could see the picture of the threat, his smile faded, and his jaw clenched. "You've got to be kidding." He returned my phone and then slammed his fist into his palm. "If this joker hurts you, he'll have to answer to me."

Detective Perkins cleared his throat. "Did Miss Winston call you? Or were you aware of the problem beforehand?"

There was no mistaking the suspicion in the detective's voice. Even after seeing J.T.'s protective reaction, did he think J.T. had hacked the monitor on purpose? A knot formed in my stomach. What if J.T. was Sharkie?

I wrapped my arms around my waist and shoved the thought aside.

"Georgia gave me a call." J.T. shook his head and held up his tablet. "I can access her monitor remotely, but I had to see this in person."

"Will you show me how the monitor works?" Detective Perkins asked.

"Sure." J.T. climbed the ladder into the combine cab and settled next to the yield monitor. Detective Perkins sat in the instructional seat. Since there wasn't room for me in the cab, I climbed the ladder and squatted on the platform. Grandpa leaned against the ladder.

J.T. worked on his tablet and explained the system to the detective. I wondered if our hovering was irritating, but he didn't seem to mind. About ten minutes later, he threw his hands up in defeat. "Everything looks completely normal, but I downloaded all the data to a flash drive. Maybe one of your tech gurus can find something I missed."

"Thanks." Detective Perkins took the flash drive. "I'll have someone take a look."

I stood aside as Detective Perkins climbed down. He paused on the ladder and looked up at me. "I'll be in touch. In the meantime, how about you do your job and let me do mine?"

I flicked my fleece's zipper tab up and down. "I'm happy to do that, seeing as how I'm not ready to meet my Maker." The truth was, the message freaked me out more than I wanted to admit.

"Good. You take care." Detective Perkins and Grandpa walked toward the road where the detective's car waited.

I stuck my head in the cab. "Am I good to go on shelling?"

"Yep." J.T. looked past me, and I followed his gaze to where the detective and Grandpa stood next to the car talking.

What if my cousin wasn't the Christian man I thought he was? No. Even though J.T. was four years younger than me, he, my brother Dakota, and I had grown up together. Our moms were sisters who were close. We'd spent lots of summer days swimming in his family's pool or in our pond. We'd built snow forts in the winter. We'd endured scorching days at the Shipshewana flea market when our moms dragged us along. I'd even watched J.T. profess his belief in Jesus Christ at his baptism ten years ago.

I flipped my braid between my fingers. "Please don't say anything about this. You know how people like to gossip."

He didn't meet my eyes. "Sure do, so you can count on me to keep my mouth shut." He gave me a light slap on the shoulder as he slipped around me and climbed down the ladder. "I'll be back to help in a few hours."

CHAPTER NINE

After a week of sunshiny days and no investigating because I didn't have a death wish, Grandpa and I finished shelling the last of the corn just a few hours before my date with Jon Nordmeyer.

Jon was better looking in person than his picture had shown, but so far that and his manners had been the only positives on this painful blind date, which led me to Life Lesson #832: Never let your stepdad fix you up. My heart squeezed as I realized Daddy would never have dreamed of sending me on a date with Jon. Not because Jon was a bad guy, but because he would've seen a mile away that this dude and I had nothing in common except that we were both Christians.

Jon caught my hand as we strolled into the theater for the musical. Really? After an hour-long drive to Indianapolis and a dinner filled with painful silences punctuated by a few babbling sessions from me, he thought it was going well enough to make a *move?* But he puffed out his chest and smirked ever so slightly. I didn't have the heart to crush him by pulling away.

I slathered on a smile and told myself that to see *Wicked,* I could tolerate hand holding.

"I'm so excited about the show," I said.

"Great." He let go of my hand and opened the door for me, and my Winston family fairness made me give him a point for chivalry. He'd already earned several. Buying dinner. Picking me up. Not being intimidated by my profession.

It's too bad a girl couldn't find a husband based on a point system alone. If that were the case, I could've closed a deal long ago.

Jon grabbed my hand again, and we found our seats—which were impressively close to the stage. As I studied the program, he rested his arm on my chair but didn't actually touch my back.

"Georgia? Is that you?" a female voice trilled.

Please, no.

Baby Kelsey sauntered down to our seats with Evan in tow. Her skinny jeans fit her perfectly and showed off her tiny legs, and her lacy, cream-colored blouse was adorable—perfect with her skin tone. If I tried to pull off that color, I'd look ill. Her perfect outfit caused me to second-guess my choice to wear skinny jeans with a black blazer.

"Hello!" I rose, and Jon did the same. While making introductions, I kept a close eye on Evan's expression for any hint of— never mind.

It was unreadable anyway.

But were his cheeks pinker than normal? Maybe he had a fever. Yeah, that would explain his choice in gir—*Nice Georgia.*

Obviously, God had more work to do with me than just my swearing problem.

"How did you two meet?" Kelsey grasped Evan's arm and leaned against him.

"One of my coworkers set us up," Jon said.

Another point to Jon for *not* mentioning my stepdad. Why

couldn't there be chemistry between us? And what was up with Kelsey? This was a totally different person than the shy girl who'd been at my house on Sunday.

"Oh, how fun. I've been wanting to see this musical for so long," Kelsey said. "It's a dream come true to experience it with the man I love."

For a second, I wanted to barf. I mean, who talks like that except for characters in bad rom-coms? Then my urge to puke passed because pity replaced it.

How sad that Kelsey felt she had to try so hard.

I smiled. "I hope you both enjoy the show."

"Thank you." Evan put his arm around Kelsey and ushered her back to their seats behind us.

The orchestra started warming up, which was perfect. I was ready to forget my troubles and get lost in the story.

During intermission, I weaved through the crowd in the theater lobby. Even if it was for only a few minutes, I said a prayer of thanks for the break from the date awkwardness.

The line for the ladies' room extended outside the door, but I didn't mind—until Evan strolled out of the men's room and right over to me.

"Are you okay?" He glanced toward the ladies' room door. "I heard about the threat on your yield monitor."

"I'm fine." I blew out a breath. Sometimes I loved living in a small town. "Who told you?"

He scrunched up his face. "The school secretary heard it from Beverly Alspaugh...who got it from Wanda Morris at the research club meeting."

Wanda was Grandpa's girlfriend and clearly the source of the family security breach. I reminded myself not to tell Grandpa any deep, dark secrets. "Are you enjoying the show?"

"Yes." His mouth drew into a thin line. "Have you thought about how serious this is?"

"No, no. I don't worry about death because I'll make a fantastic angel someday." I flipped my hair over my shoulder. How dare he cast me aside and then act like he cared?

The muscle in Evan's jaw tightened. "That's not funny. And humans don't become angels when they die."

I bristled. How could he mistake my sarcasm for theological error? "Then change the subject."

He didn't have to because Kelsey sauntered out of the ladies' room, and her eyes narrowed—just a tad—before she smiled. "Isn't the show great? I can't wait for the second act." She winked, clutched Evan's arm, and led him away.

Ugh.

"Jon did *what?*" Ashley stopped on the Wildcat Trail, and her mouth hung open as she faced me. "You're kidding, I hope."

"Um...no." I kept walking down the paved path that started at Sycamore Park, ran out of town, wound around Brandi's subdivision, and continued for approximately two and a half more miles. There, it dead-ended until town officials could raise more money to lengthen it. Part of the trail meandered through fields, and a portion snaked through a wooded area.

Like a lot of walkers, runners, and bicyclers, Ashley and I often met on Saturday mornings to exercise. Brandi normally joined us, but she was at CPR training for her school. For the past two and three-quarter miles, I'd avoided any mention of the hacked yield monitor and had opted to share about my date disaster instead.

She caught up with me and slowed to a walk. "Okay, okay. Let me see if I have this right. Kelsey and Evan were how many rows behind you?"

"Two." I pushed up my sleeves since the sun had come out, and we'd long since left the wooded portion of the trail behind.

"And it was the second act."

"Uh-huh."

She erupted into giggles. "I'm sorry, hon."

"It's not funny." I huffed as I stepped aside so a middle-aged man on a bike could pass. "How would you feel if all of a sudden your blind date leaned in for a kiss during the reprise of 'I'm Not That Girl'?" I buried my head in my hands. "Out of the corner of my eye, all I could see were giant, pursed lips coming at me—during a *live* theater production. It's not like we were a couple of teenagers in the back row of a movie theater."

Ashley guffawed—no exaggeration. A deep, manly laugh that caused the guy on the bike to gawk at us over his shoulder and almost run off the trail. "The audience didn't realize they were getting two shows for the price of one."

"You are no help." I glanced at the remains of my bean field to the left. "What if Kelsey spreads this around?" I hissed.

Ashley's expression turned serious—for about two seconds. Then she snorted.

"All right." She blew out a breath. "Kelsey probably didn't see it." She unzipped her jacket. "Does that help?"

"Do you believe what you're saying, or are you telling me that to make me feel better?"

"I plead the fifth."

"You can't do that with your friends."

"Yes, I can." She removed her jacket and tied it around her waist. "But for you, I'll keep building my case. You didn't make a big deal out of the attempted smooch, right?"

"No." When I'd leaned into the elderly lady next to me, Jon

had taken the hint and retreated. For the rest of the night, he'd sat with his hands folded in his lap. "Jon's sweet. I didn't want to embarrass him any more than he already was." Poor guy hadn't even walked me to the door when he'd dropped me off.

"Since you didn't run out of the theater screaming, I'm willing to bet Kelsey and Evan didn't notice. And so what if they did?" She shrugged.

True. It definitely wouldn't hurt Evan to know that I wasn't sitting around pining for him.

We approached the end of the trail, which was marked by a wooden barricade. About an eighth of a mile to the north stood the woods where I'd found Tara. Between the trail and the woods was a narrow strip of grass the county maintained.

Ashley studied me. "You okay? You have a funny look on your face."

I pointed to the woods. "It would've been easy for the person who killed Tara to use this trail to access my woods." I removed my phone from my pocket. "I'm going to text Detective Perkins about it—just in case."

"Georgia, this is Jon, and I've been thinking."

Oh boy. I clutched my phone, leaned against my kitchen counter, and closed my eyes, waiting for Jon to continue the message he'd left while Ashley and I had been walking.

"I don't think we're potential romantic partners."

Hallelujah.

"However, I enjoyed the time I spent with you and didn't want to leave you wondering about my intentions. Once again, I apologize for attempting to kiss you. You are quite beautiful, and while I feel physically attracted to you, our intellectual connection is lacking."

I snorted. That was an understatement.

"I wish you well, and you don't need to call me back. Unless you need closure, in which case I'd be willing to go into more detail."

Nope. Jon had summed up the date beautifully. Still, I decided to send a text.

Thanks for letting me know. I agree with your assessment and wish you the best!

I hesitated then added something else.

I have a friend you might like to meet. Let me know.

Brandi would kill me, but I'd worry about that later.

CHAPTER TEN

"What's your relationship with Evan?" Baby Kelsey pulled lip-gloss from her purse and applied it.

Yikes. How do I answer that? We were alone in the church restroom on Sunday morning. I started washing my hands and gazed at the bags under my eyes that made me look every day of thirty—and more. Still, I took some consolation in my new navy dress with gold grommets on the sleeves and hem. "We're just friends." I brushed a bit of lint from my skirt.

Doubt flitted across her overly-made-up face, and her eyes narrowed. "Really." She placed her lip-gloss tube back in her clutch and snapped it shut. "I don't believe you."

"Is that why you suggested a double date?"

She faced me. "You and Evan were deep in conversation Friday night during intermission. Plus, I've seen the way you look at him."

"Have you noticed the way he looks at *you?*"

Her mouth flattened.

I took that as a *no*, pushed on the paper towel dispenser, and ripped off a sheet. Rock solid, eh? Why was I always trying to be

Nice Georgia? The one everybody would like? Clearly, it wasn't working. Telling the truth in this moment was doing me absolutely no good because it was obvious she was looking for trouble.

I'd tell her what she wanted to hear. I was after all, at my core, a people pleaser. A failed one, but a pleaser nonetheless.

I shook my head slowly. "You're right. I'll be honest since you're so good at sniffing out the truth. Evan and I have always had a special bond." I lowered my voice. "For a while, I thought God was telling me he was the one." I shrugged. "I guess I was wrong... Unless I wasn't. In which case, your days are numbered." I wiped my hands and chucked the wadded paper past Baby Kelsey's head and into the garbage. "You never know what complications God might use to bring people together." I winked and patted her on the shoulder. "Catch you at small group tonight."

Her face crumpled, and I sailed out of the restroom.

And ran right into Detective Perkins. Literally. I plowed into him.

He steadied me, and his hands lingered on my upper arms. "Excuse me."

"No. Excuse *me*." Heat crept into my face. "How are you, Detective?"

The restroom door whooshed open, and a red-eyed Kelsey charged out. She flew past us but then turned and stomped back. "Cal, I swear, you'd better stay away from her. She's nothing but trouble—and she just told me, she's already met *the one*." She smirked and sashayed away in her black leather mini.

Had Detective Perkins dated Kelsey too? How was it possible this child I could've babysat—if I'd ever been the babysitting type—was singlehandedly ruining my life? "How do you know Kelsey?"

He chuckled. "She's my cousin."

Of course she was. Here in the good ol' heartland, everybody was related to everybody else—which was another reason my prospects were limited. I wondered about the detective, but Beverly would surely know if we were kin.

"Is she right? Have you met the one?"

"Nope. I was telling her what she wanted to hear."

"Right." His brow furrowed, and he studied me. "Thanks for the text about the Wildcat Trail."

"It's probably crazy."

"No. It's a good thought. I checked to see if the security cameras caught who parked in that area, but all the cameras are pointed at the playground equipment and gazebo instead of the trailhead. But tomorrow, I'll follow up and see if any of the regulars noticed someone different using the trail that morning."

I nodded as music blasted through the sanctuary's open doors. "We'd better get going."

"You want to grab some lunch after the service?"

Whoa. I hadn't expected that. Good thing I'd decided to wear my new dress. "Um. Sure. That sounds great." At least I might be able to find out information on the investigation.

He grinned. "Cool. And feel free to call me Cal."

Cal and I found a table next to the window at Velda's Café after we'd ordered. The restaurant was a popular place to gather after church on Sundays. The shop had a vintage chic look with mismatched tables and chairs. Historical photos taken all around Wildcat Springs hung on the soft yellow walls.

Though my first instinct had been that this lunch outing might allow me to ask questions about Daddy's murder investigation and Tara's case, I'd decided during Pastor Mark's sermon on patience that I should wait for Cal to bring them up.

At least I was self-aware enough to know that wouldn't be easy.

"Did you grow up in this area?" I rolled the straw paper between my fingers.

"Nope. Solon, Ohio—Cleveland suburb."

"How'd you end up here?"

"I have extended family in this area, and when I was a kid, my grandma used to talk about how great it was growing up on a farm."

"Beverly's sister?"

"Right. My grandma was the oldest girl in her family and passed away a couple of years ago." He swallowed. "After three years on the police force in Cleveland, I started wanting something simpler. A house in the country—or a small hobby farm." He glanced out the window and then met my eyes. "With the hours I've been putting in at work, I don't have time for a garden or chickens." He folded his hands. "How'd you end up farming?"

"My brother didn't have an interest, and I did—though I didn't admit it until after Daddy died and Grandpa started talking about selling our farm. I was going to be a music teacher." I shook my head. "Until I student taught and realized God didn't equip me to deal with a classroom full of antsy kiddos—no matter what age they are."

Cal leaned back and chuckled. "I couldn't deal with that either."

"I had a quarter-life crisis of epic proportions while I was student teaching. I knew God would show me something else to do with my life, but I never thought it'd be farming without my dad." I took a deep breath, and Cal reached for my hand.

The bell on the door jingled, and Kelsey strutted in with Evan. I withdrew my hand.

"Cal!" She squealed and hurried over with more enthusiasm than I'd ever seen her demonstrate. "I hope you don't mind if we join you. I told Evan we *had* to come over because I was dying for some of Velda's vegetable soup."

"Sure. Go ahead and order," Cal said. "As you can see, we're still waiting." They left to get in line. "Sorry. Kelsey means well."

"She has a weird way of showing it." I leaned back, crossed my arms, and marveled at her miraculous recovery after our restroom encounter.

Cal's laughter boomed through the café, and for a second, its resonance reminded me of Daddy's laugh.

Even though I wanted to claw Kelsey's eyes out, I decided to spin this situation positively. "Getting to know Evan would be nice for you," I said. "We're in the same Bible study group. You're always welcome."

"That's not my thing."

"How come?"

"A lot of them are social groups—no spiritual substance. Then there's the sharing private feelings thing."

"Nobody makes you share more than you want, and we just finished a study of Ecclesiastes. We're meeting at Evan's place tonight if you change your mind."

"Thanks." He shifted and glanced out at the traffic streaming by on Main Street.

I tried not to take offense and told myself his declining my invitation didn't make him any less of a Christian. "What are your feelings about church?"

"Wildcat Springs Community? Or church in general?"

"Both."

A server brought our food. Cal offered to pray, and when the food was blessed, I waited for him to answer.

"Your church is fine," he said. "Friendly -I felt welcome."

"But?" I tore a piece of sour dough from the lid to my bread bowl and tossed it into my chicken noodle soup.

"I'm not sure it's where I'm going to land. But then again,

your church may be the best option around, so I haven't ruled it out."

"Oh my goodness, Georgia. How can you eat so many carbs?" Kelsey sat next to me and wrinkled her nose. Evan was paying for their meals.

"I hate feeling hungry all the time." I was *not* going to let her get to me. *Nice Georgia.*

"I can tell."

Cal frowned. "Easy, Kels."

I shrugged. "There's more to life than being skinny. You have to enjoy a good piece of pie once in a while." I surveyed the pies Velda had displayed in the case by the door. I'd have to pass on a slice of chocolate silk today—my pride was worth something.

Kelsey followed my gaze. "That's what fat people say."

"Is it?" I grinned. "How enlightening. Do you speak from experience?"

"No." She scowled and clutched the edge of the table. "I've *never* been overweight."

"I apologize," I said. "You seem so knowledgeable and disciplined when it comes to nutrition."

She fiddled with her silver earring. "Thanks."

Evan took the seat next to Kelsey. "What'd I miss?"

Cal cleared his throat. "A fascinating discussion about nutrition."

Evan took Kelsey's hand and squeezed. "My girl has taught me so much about eating right. I never thought I could cut back on meat, but I've been doing it."

"Pretty soon, you'll be a vegetarian like me." She gazed into his eyes.

He beamed.

Life Lesson #327: Love did conquer all. Including the desire to eat meat—but I'd believe that when I saw it. If Evan could give up his love for wings, I'd eat nothing but tofu for a month.

The waiter brought their food, and Kelsey eyed the sandwich on Evan's plate. "Is that *turkey?*"

The tips of his ears flamed. "I thought it'd be okay since we had vegetarian last night."

She pursed her lips. "Whatev."

Cal and I exchanged glances. We needed a redo on this hijacked date.

"Be honest," Cal said as we stood in the public parking lot down the street from Velda's Café after Evan and Kelsey had left. "What's the history with you and Evan?"

"Is this the detective talking or my new friend?" I crossed my arms and leaned against my truck.

He grinned. "Both."

"We've always just been friends. For a while I thought it might be more, but..." A brisk wind whipped through my thin raincoat.

"It didn't work out?"

"Right. It's fine, though. I want him to be happy."

"That's sweet of you, but my cousin's behavior is probably making that hard for you to accept."

"You got me." Why, oh why, did I have to be so easy to read?

"No, I get it. She has a good heart. I'm not sure why she's acting so insecure."

"She's young." I shrugged. "Are you coming to group tonight?"

"Probably not." He ran his fingers through his hair. "But I'd like to see you again. How about Saturday?"

I smiled. "Deal."

"And Georgia?"

"Yeah?"

"I haven't forgotten about your dad's case. With the Fullerton investigation, it's been crazy, but as soon as we wrap that up, I'll finish going through his file."

I'd hoped for something bigger, but when I'd put the situation in the Lord's hands three years ago, I'd had to surrender the timing, though I wasn't a fan of how long it was taking. "How *is* the Fullerton case?"

He grimaced. "We're hoping to make an arrest soon."

That afternoon while I sprawled on my sectional sofa and watched the Colts game on TV, my phone dinged with a text from Jon Nordmeyer.

Tell me more about your friend.

I sent him a few details about Brandi. She might hate the idea, but dipping her toes in the dating waters wouldn't be dangerous with someone like Jon as long as he'd learned his lesson and would keep his lips to himself.

He'd done everything else right on the date. They'd at least have a pleasant conversation because Brandi was good at drawing people out. Now, I needed to tell Ashley not to say anything to Brandi about the almost kiss.

My phone chimed again.

Sounds good. If she approves, please send me her number.

I should show Brandi the dossier Dan had created. I flipped my braid between my fingers and bit my lip. Even without her knowing the whole story of my date, getting Brandi's approval would be difficult.

97

That evening our small group gathered at Evan's modest ranch house in Sycamore Hills, the same subdivision where Brandi lived. I stood in his kitchen and squirted a healthy amount of spicy ketchup on the lettuce-wrapped black bean burger that New and Improved Evan—with Kelsey's assistance—had prepared.

In all the years I'd known him, he'd never so much as offered a vegetarian option, let alone made it the sole entrée. Old Evan would've offered a choice of burgers, hot dogs, or brats along with the appropriate sides and condiments.

Nevertheless, I was willing to try something new and prove to Kelsey that I wasn't afraid of her food.

I took my paper plate, also filled with carrot sticks and hummus, to the living room that was open to the kitchen. J.T. and Dave were engrossed in a Broncos game. Ashley was deep in conversation with Heather, so I sat next to Brandi on the leather sofa.

"How was lunch with Cal?" She swiped a red pepper in the hummus.

"How did you find out about that?"

"Before you got here, Evan mentioned the four of you ate lunch together and that he invited Cal to come tonight. I think Evan was hoping Cal would show, so there'd be another guy."

Before I could comment or ask her about a potential date with Jon, a commotion in the kitchen interrupted.

"I told you we didn't need dessert," Kelsey hissed.

Brandi and I whipped around and gawked at her.

Kelsey pointed at a stack of pink boxes from Pastry Delight sitting on Evan's island. "When did you get those?"

"Yesterday afternoon. They were out in the garage fridge." A stain of red crept up Evan's neck as he removed a chocolate silk pie from a box and set it on the counter next to a peanut butter cream pie. "My friends like pie." His tone was tense, like he was trying to keep everyone from staring at them—which was completely unsuccessful.

Except for J.T., who was worried about the Broncos. Too bad he didn't have the same devotion to the Colts. It would've saved me from hearing Evan extol the wonders of Kelsey at our gathering earlier in the month.

"You never listen to me." Kelsey put her hands on her hips.

Evan furrowed his brow. "About what?"

"The dangers of sugar. Fat. Carbs. Obesity."

I dipped a carrot in hummus, popped it in my mouth, and sat back to watch the show.

"Sweetie, this isn't the time or place." He took out a sugar cream pie.

"Don't *sweetie* me." She glanced over her shoulder at all of us, then turned back. "Admit it. You bought them for *her*." She hitched her thumb over her shoulder.

Okay, so assuming the *her* in question was me, due to our earlier conversation about pie, why in the name of all that's holy, would she make that accusation in front of everyone?

"That's ridiculous," Evan said. "Everyone in this group likes pie."

"Yeah, pie's kind of our group's thing." Heather got up off the couch and tossed her plate and napkin in the trash.

J.T. looked up. "It's true. Peanut butter's my favorite."

So he did have an awareness that extended beyond the game.

"I'm a fan of cherry," Dave said as he adjusted his baseball cap.

"I'm partial to peach," Ashley drawled.

"And I like chocolate silk." Brandi elbowed me. Did she expect me to chime in with a pie that wasn't a current option?

"I've always liked mince." I cleared my throat to stifle a giggle as Brandi rolled her eyes.

"See, it's all perfectly innocent." Evan rubbed Kelsey's shoulder.

"Yeah, right." Kelsey jerked away, picked up the chocolate silk pie, raised it above her head, and chucked it in the trash. Then, she ran into the bathroom and slammed the door.

Whoa. Any amusement I'd felt over Kelsey's tantrum vanished.

Heather's eyes were humongous. Ashley gasped, and Brandi's mouth hung open.

Evan wiped a blob of whipped cream from his cheek and licked his finger.

"Touchdown!" J.T. shot off the couch and did a hip-bumping victory dance with Dave.

Evan started toward the bathroom, stopped, and looked back. "I'm so sorry, guys. We'd agreed to have a healthy meal, and I thought that meant we could have dessert."

"Apparently not." I surveyed the remaining pies sitting on the counter. "But *we* can eat the peanut butter and sugar cream, right?"

CHAPTER ELEVEN

O n Monday, I woke up later than usual and trudged through the living room into my kitchen because I hadn't been able to sleep after the excitement of The Pie Incident.

Evan had banged on the bathroom door and tried to coax Kelsey out, but she refused. So, he divided the offending pies among us and sent us on our way with profuse apologies that we weren't having our lesson and prayer time. After the awkwardness, no one had appeared to mind, and we definitely knew what we needed to pray about.

My head pounded from lack of caffeine, so I brewed coffee and took a survey of my pantry contents. Jars of green beans Mom and I had canned from my garden, salsa Mom had made from my tomatoes, fruit cocktail, a box of outdated wild rice, and a bag of tortilla chips filled with crumbs. My refrigerator wasn't any better. Ranch dressing, ketchup, and peanut butter cream pie.

The pie won.

I poured a cup of coffee and dug into the slice. It was too bad Kelsey thought she couldn't trust Evan, which is what that little incident had to have been about. No one who was secure in a relationship got that upset over pies.

I hoped Evan knew what he was getting into. Did his training as a counselor make him think he could fix her insecurities? Kelsey's behavior was a huge red flag because if she would act like that when they were dating, what might she do if they tied the knot?

God, give Evan wisdom. Help Kelsey not to be so insecure.

After downing a cup of coffee and polishing off the pie, the caffeine began to hit my brain, and it became clear I needed to spend some time at the grocery store, so I got ready and headed to Hometown Market in downtown Wildcat Springs. Brandi always said I needed to be prepared in case of a natural or man-made disaster because she might not have enough supplies for everyone who'd probably show up at her house.

That was the advantage of *not* being a prepper—no one would dream of descending on my house in the midst of the apocalypse.

I was picking out bananas when Evan stopped beside me.

"Aren't you supposed to be at work?" I located a small bunch with plenty of green and put it in my cart.

"Fall break."

"Are you sure it's safe to be seen with me?" *Why had I said that?*

The muscle in his jaw twitched. "Kelsey and I broke up."

"I'm so sorry." I tightened my grip on the cart.

"Are you?" His voice held a note of accusation.

I wasn't heartless, but his tone irked me. "What's that supposed to mean?" I started walking toward the apples, and Evan followed.

"Does your encounter in the church restroom ring a bell?"

My face flamed, but I faced him anyway. "She was goading me, so I spouted off. I didn't mean any of it." I surveyed the apples. "Don't blame Kelsey's insecurity on me." I heaved a bag of Honeycrisps off the display.

"I know." He sighed. "It was never enough. No matter what I did." He pointed to his cart. "Look at all these fruits and vegetables."

"And steak." The package of meat was half-hidden under a bag of spinach.

He ignored my comment and held up a bunch of broccoli. "She's still in my head. I never touched broccoli before we dated."

"You don't have to torture yourself."

"I actually like it."

I quirked an eyebrow. "Torture?"

He rolled his eyes. "*Broccoli.*"

Good to know. "I could talk to Kelsey."

"Oh, no." His eyes widened. "Don't do that."

"But if she knew there wasn't anything between you and me, then—"

"Georgia, leave it alone."

"How can I? You're blaming me."

"I was venting. Sorry." He lowered his voice. "Kels and I obviously weren't as rock solid as I thought, so I don't know if I want to go there again..." He shoved his hands in his pockets. "Please don't say anything."

I sighed. "Fine. I just hate seeing you upset."

"I'll survive."

I pointed to his cart. "Yeah, you'll outlive all of us when you're eating like that."

———

"This bouquet is lovely, dearie. You have great taste," Beverly Alspaugh said.

After I'd unloaded my groceries at home, I'd set out for Beverly's place, down the road from my farmhouse.

"Thank you. I thought they'd cheer you up." I perched on her flowered couch while her black Schnauzer, Miss Peacock, pawed my legs.

"Certainly." Beverly drew her robe tighter, settled in her recliner, and pulled a blanket over her legs, even though the room was stuffy.

"How are you feeling?" I ignored the dog and hoped she'd realize I was the Alpha and leave me alone. Instead, she gave a yippy bark and attempted to leap onto the couch.

"Down, Miss Peacock," Beverly said. The dog actually obeyed, sat next to the couch, and gazed up at me.

I patted her head. So much for being the Alpha.

"Not terrible. Cancer's not going to take me before the good Lord's ready, so I rest in that."

I wasn't sure I'd be able to rest. I'd probably be kicking and screaming while the angel of death dragged me away.

The creases in Beverly's forehead deepened. "Are you okay? Finding Tara couldn't have been easy."

I swallowed. "It definitely brought back memories of Daddy's death."

"Of all people in Wildcat Springs to have found Tara." Beverly shook her head. "I've been praying for years for your dad's case to be solved. Sometimes I wonder what the good Lord's thinking, letting a killer roam free, and now there's another one." Miss Peacock darted to Beverly, and she reached down and scooped her up. "But, I always remind myself to trust God. He'll reveal the truth in the proper time."

"Your great-nephew may help things along."

Beverly clasped her hands. "Wonderful. I pray for him all the time. When I was growing up, I never thought I'd see the day when we had murders in our little town." She shook her head.

104

"I'm thankful Tara knew Jesus. I've often wondered if her mother did."

I couldn't ignore an opening like that. "How did you know Tara and her mom?"

"They stayed with me after they moved to town around sixteen years ago. Your family's rental house wasn't going to be ready for a couple of weeks because of a water leak, so your daddy asked if I could put them up."

"What was Tara like?"

Beverly looked out the window and stroked Miss Peacock's head. I followed her gaze. One tree still had leaves—a stubborn hold out. "Tara was sweet to me, but she wasn't always respectful to her mama, and it didn't help her dad was never in the picture. If she'd have been my daughter, I'd have jerked a knot in her tail."

I grinned. Beverly's bluntness was one of the reasons I loved her. "Had you seen Tara recently?"

"She came to see me a few weeks ago. Told me she'd found Jesus. Seems she was having boy trouble and needed advice. Ever since her mama died, Tara didn't have many people to confide in."

"What was wrong?"

Beverly hesitated and fiddled with her blanket but took a deep breath and continued. "She'd met a new fellow and wasn't sure how to break it off with her current beau without making him angry."

"And the current beau was Mike Dunson?"

"I believe so."

"Did she happen to call the new boyfriend Sharkie?"

Beverly squinted at the ceiling. "She didn't call him anything."

Of course not. "Was Tara afraid for her life?"

"I didn't think so at the time."

"Did you tell Cal?"

"Soon as I heard her death was ruled a homicide, this old brain started chugging away, so I called him." Beverly's eyes gleamed. "I see you're on a first name basis with him."

"We may or may not have gone to lunch after church yesterday." I winked.

"Praise the Lord!" When Beverly raised her hands, Miss Peacock shot off her lap, and attacked my leg again. "Down, Miss Peacock!"

The dog obeyed and went to sit at Beverly's feet as my phone started vibrating. I was going to ignore it, but Beverly motioned for me to go ahead.

"Hello?"

"Georgia? It's J.T."

"What's up?"

"About an hour ago, Detective Perkins came into the store and questioned me about Tara Fullerton's death."

I blinked a few times as I ran my hand over Beverly's couch. "Why?"

"Because I was with Tara the morning she died."

CHAPTER TWELVE

An hour later, armed with two turkey club sandwiches, a large order of homemade potato chips, and two raspberry iced teas from Velda's Café, I located an empty—and isolated—picnic table in the sun near the grove of trees that surrounded the backside of Sycamore Park and waited for J.T. to arrive. Before ending our phone call, I'd promised to meet him and bring him lunch. Though my voice had been strained, my offer had sounded far more gracious than I was feeling now that the shock had worn off and allowed me time to stew.

Swiping crunchy leaves from the faded red table and bench, I fumed. J.T. had lied about his relationship with Tara.

Whatever his reasons, I *would* get to the bottom of this. I sat at the table and waited.

Since the school was on fall break, a few kids played on the swings, monkey bars, and slides a short distance from where I'd camped out. The public pool was closed for the season, and it managed to look downright lonely with a padlocked gate, stacked chairs, and a cover.

"Hey, cuz." There was no mistaking the defeat in J.T.'s voice as he lumbered up to me.

I motioned to the seat across from me. "Sit." I couldn't mask the irritation in my tone.

He obeyed and met my gaze. "I didn't hurt Tara," he whispered and scrubbed his hands over his face. "She was alive—and safe—when I left."

"So you're a suspect?"

He swallowed. "Yeah. I think so."

Obviously, Cal didn't have enough to arrest J.T., or he would've. Still, Cal had been on a fishing expedition to see what he could get on my cousin. Pushing that thought aside, I folded my hands and rested them on the paint-chipped wood. "If you were with Tara the morning she died, then you lied to me about your relationship with her." My head pounded with multiple cuss words that begged for release. "Why?"

"We'd started hanging out again and decided to go hunting because I'd mentioned I hadn't been for years."

Now I knew why Tara had been on my land without permission. J.T. had a standing invitation to use my woods—and Daddy's old tree stand. "Doesn't explain the lie." I pressed my lips together.

"I'm getting there. That morning I told her I wanted to be exclusive. That's when she told me about her boyfriend Mike and that she wanted to stay with him because she thought he was close to accepting Christ. Tara was afraid if she broke up with him, he'd stop going to church and forget about God." He sighed. "It sounded like a lame excuse to get rid of me."

Cheating on your boyfriend but staying with him so he'll get saved. That's a good one. But Tara had been a new Christian, so maybe I was being too hard on her. "And you had this little define-the-relationship-chat-turned-argument while you were *hunting?*"

"Yes. I was an idiot for ever thinking we could be more than friends." He covered his face with his hands. "After we argued, I needed to get away and cool off—besides I had to work."

"How'd you get home?"

"I walked."

J.T. lived about a mile and a half from the scene. "Did you see any strange vehicles parked where they shouldn't have been?"

He set his jaw. "No."

"Anyone on the Wildcat Trail?"

"I couldn't see from the stand, so I have no idea. Probably." He frowned. "And when I left, I walked in the opposite direction of the trail."

"Right." Since he lived that way it made sense.

He fixed his gaze on a squirrel scampering up a tree. "I know it looks bad."

"No kidding, *Sharkie*." I rolled my eyes. "Don't you think you should've called a lawyer before you talked to Detective Perkins? Are you *trying* to go to prison?"

"Detective Perkins came into the store and took me by surprise." He squeezed his hands together. "I didn't want to make a scene, and if I got a lawyer, I'd look guilty. I didn't have anything to hide."

I sighed and massaged my temples before meeting his gaze. "I'm sorry you lost Tara—and that this is happening." He nodded, and I slid his turkey sandwich across the table, opened the bag of chips, and positioned it between us. "What do they have on you?"

"Text messages that show we planned to hunt that morning. My prints are all over her crossbow because I carried it for her. And obviously, I don't have an alibi."

"Anything else?" I crunched down on a potato chip that contained a hint of garlic mingled with the salt.

"Well, they think I could've hacked your yield monitor."

"And make yourself look guiltier? Yeah, that makes sense."

He shook his head and compressed his lips. "That's what I thought, but I didn't say that to Detective Perkins." He gazed over my shoulder for a second before he picked up his sandwich and took a bite.

God had clearly blessed my cousin with more self-control than he'd seen fit to give me. While I ate, I thought back over everything I'd observed at the scene, and the locked car came to mind because it bugged me. If Tara's car had a keypad, then locking her keys in the car wouldn't have been a big deal, but it didn't.

"Did Tara realize she'd locked her keys in her car that morning?"

J.T. frowned. "What?" He put down his sandwich. "No. In fact, she said she was going to leave the car unlocked and her keys in the ignition because she knew the car would be safe back where we parked."

"You had an actual conversation about it?"

"Yeah." He tilted his head. "Why?"

"When Grandpa and I found Tara's car, the doors were all locked."

"Neither one of us did it. We double checked before we left." He took a drink of tea. "Somebody came along and locked the doors? Why?"

"Could Tara have had something in her car that the killer wanted?"

"And after taking it, the killer accidentally locked the doors out of habit."

"Right. Do you remember seeing anything unusual in the car?"

J.T. closed his eyes, and a moment later opened them. "No. But that doesn't mean anything. I was nervous about asking her to be exclusive."

Another possibility came to mind. "What if someone planted

something in Tara's car? Did Detective Perkins mention anything they found?"

"No." J.T. looked older than his twenty-six years, which was *not* something I would've said about him two weeks ago.

We ate in silence, the only sounds coming from passing cars and the giggles and shouts of playing kiddos. "I'm going to talk to Detective Perkins and see what I can find out."

"Thanks." He walked to the trash barrel, tossed his sandwich wrapper inside, and returned to our table as the sun ducked behind a cloud, the shadow darkening our table.

"Why'd Tara call you *Sharkie?*"

J.T. picked a paint chip from the table. "Back in my marching band days, we'd play cards to pass the time on bus trips. I was good at all of them except Euchre, which Tara loved. She took to calling me Sharkie—like a card shark—because I could never remember the rules." He flicked the paint chip into the grass. "It sounds cruel, but she didn't mean it that way." He blinked as if he were trying to keep tears away.

"Did you have a nickname for her?"

"T-Full." He shrugged. "Not super creative, but she never minded."

I wadded up my sandwich wrapper and the empty potato chip bag and clutched them. There was one thing more I had to know. "Why'd you lie to me about your relationship with Tara?" This time, the anger had left my voice.

He fiddled with his shirt collar. "I'm embarrassed that she'd been seeing another guy the whole time I was pursuing her. But mostly, I felt guilty for leaving her alone. If I'd been there to protect her, she'd still be alive."

I nodded as goosebumps rose on my arms. "Or you might be dead too."

As soon as J.T. left for work, I drove straight to the sheriff's department to see Cal.

"Is Detective Perkins available?" I asked the receptionist after she'd given me the once over.

She chuckled and flipped her bangs out of her eyes. She picked up her phone. "Georgia Winston, right?"

"Yes, ma'am."

She sniffed as she pressed in Cal's extension. "Georgia Winston's here to see you." She listened for a second before replacing the phone in its cradle. "He'll be out in a few."

"That's a cute top." I pointed to her blouse with flowing sleeves. "Purple's your color."

"Thanks." She shot a fake, half smile in my direction.

So much for trying to be Nice Georgia. When would I ever learn it never worked?

A few minutes later, I heard someone whistling "Stayin' Alive," and Cal opened the door. "Come on back." As I passed, he whispered, "You look gorgeous."

"Thanks." When I couldn't manage to return his smile, his friendly expression faded.

"What's going on?" he asked.

"Is there some place we could speak in private?"

"No problem." He turned left and led me down a narrow hallway, opened a door, and stood aside so I could enter the room, which held a desk with a chair and two additional chairs that faced each other. An observation mirror dominated the opposite wall.

"I should've expected an interrogation room when I asked for privacy."

He chuckled and indicated that I should sit, so I did.

"What's on your mind?" he asked.

"J.T. Simms is my cousin." My statement hung in the air, and the interrogation room seemed to shrink, squeezing the air out of my chest.

Cal nodded slowly, and I couldn't read his expression. "I see," he said.

"There's no way he killed Tara Fullerton. He's one of the kindest people I know." I clutched my purse handle. "When his mom had a car accident a few years ago, he and my uncle took turns staying with her in the hospital. They never left her side, and Aunt Janie swears J.T. took such good care of her, he could've been a nurse." J.T.'d never speak to me again if he knew I was spouting off about his tenderhearted side, but he'd have to get over it because this was a desperate situation.

"I've just been following the evidence in this investigation." Cal looked away.

"Okay. Well, I have a question about that." I dropped my purse on the floor. "Why would J.T. hack my yield monitor and then hand you the evidence?"

Cal shook his head. "You'd be surprised what people think they can get away with. Besides, when he showed up, I was there. It would've looked suspicious if he hadn't cooperated."

"What about Mike Dunson? He could've hacked my yield monitor."

Cal swiped his hand over his mouth and chin. "I hate this, but I have to go with what the evidence is showing, and right now it points to J.T.—not Mike Dunson."

"Then there's something you missed." There had to be. J.T. wouldn't threaten me. He wouldn't have hurt Tara. "Did you ever follow up with the regulars who use the Wildcat Trail?"

"No one remembers seeing anyone new that morning. I'm sorry." Sincerity filled his tone.

"What about motive?" I folded my arms.

"I'm not done digging, but J.T.'s already admitted they fought about Mike the morning Tara died."

"J.T. should've had a lawyer present when you talked to him."

Cal crossed his arms. "Your cousin wasn't under arrest when I spoke with him, which I have the right to do." His blue eyes grew cold.

"It feels like you tricked him into talking."

He stood and turned away from me. "What if you're wrong, Georgia?" He faced me and leaned against the chair back. "Are you sure you know J.T. as well as you think you do?"

Pressing my fist to my mouth, I considered Cal's argument. There was a major piece that didn't fit with the man I knew. "Fine. Let's say you're right and J.T. pushed Tara off the stand in the heat of the moment—either accidentally or on purpose. If the fall had caused her death, I'd be inclined to agree with you." I leaned forward. "But here's what I don't buy. Instead of J.T. calling for help, he *suffocated* her?" I shook my head. "J.T.'s not that kind of man. Besides, someone else was at the scene. After I found Tara, I looked at her car, and all the doors were locked. J.T. told me they left them *unlocked* because the keys were in the ignition." I stood and picked up my purse. "You've got the wrong guy, and meanwhile, there's a murderer running free."

Cal pressed his lips together, as if he wanted to say more but decided against it and opened the door. We walked the narrow hall in silence, and when we arrived at the exit to the waiting room, he rested his hand on my shoulder and sympathy filled his eyes. "I'm sorry, but I think we should cancel our date on Saturday."

"I understand." The cynical edge in those two simple words of agreement speared my heart.

Cal turned to go but then faced me. "Take care, Georgia. I'll be in touch about your dad's case."

As I watched him walk away, I thought about Life Lesson #6: When it comes to men, never get your hopes up.

Ever.

CHAPTER THIRTEEN

A few years ago, I'd gotten a decorating burr under my tail and had spent a ridiculous amount of time online looking for ideas to improve my farmhouse. I'd decided that a chalkboard painted on my dining room wall would be cool, so I'd made a trip to Mitchell's Hardware in Wildcat Springs and asked for the special paint. Harry, the grizzled man who ran the place, had guffawed himself into a coughing fit, spat into his hanky, and said, "I don't sell that newfangled stuff here."

Undeterred, but fuming at the people who pontificated on the necessity of shopping local, I'd driven to Richardville, purchased the paint, and created a plain black rectangle on the light blue wall above the sideboard in my dining room. I'd found some narrow pieces of reclaimed wood and trimmed the chalkboard out, but because I don't have an artistic cell in my body, this little production was about as crafty as I got. Every so often, Ashley would draw a picture to spruce up the board.

Her latest creation was a Pomeranian, which was her way of reminding me that I needed a pet. Since she'd drawn the dog in the corner, I had a large blank area that I could use for my murder investigation board. After my encounter with Cal, I needed to keep my mind occupied, so I stood in front of the wall in my dining room with a piece of chalk in hand and bit my lip. I had to solve this case to help my cousin. Where should I start?

A timeline.

I drew a line across the board, and on the left end, I put a vertical mark and noted Tara's approximate time of death and the time I'd discovered her body. On the wood frame, I tacked up printed social media pictures of Tara and the people I'd interviewed: Nick Vogler, Mike Dunson, Kevin Doyle, and Pam Marconi. Under each person's name, I wrote the facts I'd learned. Then, I added Morgan Hopewood's picture because I wanted to talk to her.

When I finished, I dropped the chalk in the basket on the sideboard, surveyed my results—and decided it was time to follow up with Nick Vogler.

After I found his card in my handbag, I leaned against the dining room table and hoped I could leave a message, but he answered. I reminded him who I was and how we'd met.

He remembered.

"May I ask a few more questions?" I asked.

"Not unless you let me buy you dinner."

I gripped the edge of the table. That was *not* what I'd had in mind, but it might yield better results. "When?"

"How about tomorrow night?"

"Sure." At least it was a weeknight deal, so he wasn't taking it too seriously.

We arranged a time and place, and when I hung up, I squeezed my eyes shut. I needed to talk to my girls, so I pulled out my phone and sent an SOS text to Brandi and Ashley.

Twenty minutes later, Brandi arrived with a plate of fresh chocolate chip cookies, which was her usual contribution when I sent a distress message. "What's wrong?"

I took the plate. "J.T.'s a suspect in Tara Fullerton's murder. Detective Perkins questioned him today."

"You're kidding."

"I wish." *For so many reasons.*

"Well, obviously he didn't kill her." But there was a flicker of doubt in her eyes as she removed her denim jacket, folded it, and placed it on the bench in the foyer.

Ashley, dressed in workout clothes, breezed through the front door. "Guess what I just saw?"

Brandi and I exchanged glances. Ashley was way too giddy for the news to be about J.T.

"What?" I closed the door.

"Kelsey posted on Facebook about being single, so she and Evan must've broken up."

"Uh-oh." Brandi's eyes were wide.

"They did," I said. "I saw Evan at the grocery store today, and he told me."

Ashley unzipped her sweatshirt and tossed it on the bench. "I can't say I'm shocked. I've never seen a grown woman behave like she did—unless it was for cameras on a reality TV show."

Brandi cleared her throat.

"I know." Ashley held up her hands. "We shouldn't gossip."

"Are you still hoping you have a chance with Evan?" The crease in Brandi's forehead deepened.

"Right now, I have more on my mind than Evan Beckworth." I headed for the kitchen and hoped the topic at hand would keep them from noticing my murder investigation board in the dining room. "Besides, I'm moving beyond Evan." If I said the words out loud, I might really mean them. I set the plate of cookies on the counter, opened a cabinet, and pulled out three glasses.

"Because of Jon?" Brandi asked.

I needed to tell her about Jon and the text I'd sent about him meeting her. "No. He's a great guy, but there was zero chemistry."

"Chemistry isn't everything," Brandi said.

I glared at her as I picked up a cookie. "You want me to settle?" I shoved the whole thing in my mouth.

Ashley rested her hand on my shoulder. "Absolutely not. No man is better than the wrong man."

"Amen," Brandi added.

That had to be Life Lesson #1. Well, knowing and walking with Jesus ought to come first, so the man thing should be pushed down to #3. Still, it surprised me to hear Ashley say that since she'd always seemed so boy crazy.

"What about Cal?" Ashley leaned against the island.

My heart clenched. "That's not going to work out." I walked to the refrigerator and grabbed the milk.

"Why not, hon?" Ashley raised her eyebrows. "Please tell me you didn't push away that fine specimen of a man."

What a nice vote of confidence. "He's pegged J.T. as a suspect in Tara Fullerton's murder, so he canceled. You know, it doesn't look good dating a suspect's cousin."

Ashley gasped. "What? No! J.T.?"

While I poured milk, I told them everything I'd learned from J.T. and included my story of confronting Cal. I rolled my eyes. "Usually the guys I date meet the girl they marry after paying attention to me. A potential love interest looking to arrest a relative is new territory."

"I'm so sorry." Brandi said. "Let's pray about it. Right now."

I nodded, and we circled up. Brandi asked God to give J.T. strength and to make the truth known.

When she finished, Ashley huffed. "I can't believe it. J.T. wouldn't kill anyone. He's harmless." She picked up a cookie and started nibbling, and I wondered if there was more to Ashley's reaction than friendly concern. For a while, I'd suspected that she had her eye on J.T.

"I'm going to prove he's being set up." I took two more cookies and sat at the table. "J.T. swears when he left the woods that day Tara was alive and well, and I believe him. Whoever Tara wanted to investigate killed her and hoped it would look like an accident, but when I turned in the letter and the police ruled her death a homicide, the killer decided to set J.T. up. The problem is, J.T. hasn't done anything illegal that Tara would've found suspicious."

"What do you mean?" Brandi asked.

"If Tara was killed because she found dirt that someone wanted to keep hidden, then it doesn't make sense that J.T. killed her. The only motive Detective Perkins has is a lover's spat between J.T. and Tara."

Brandi nodded. "Which is probably why J.T. hasn't been arrested."

"Yep."

"I want to help," Ashley said.

Brandi bit her lip. "I'd tell you to let the police handle it, but they've done a lousy job so far. Will you promise you won't do anything stupid? Or run around by yourself?"

Considering the threat on my yield monitor, that wasn't a bad idea. "I promise." Then I remembered my date with Nick Vogler. Since I didn't know him, our upcoming outing could be classified as stupid. "How would you both like to be my spies tomorrow night?"

On Tuesday, Grandpa and I tilled soil in some of our fields, and late that afternoon, I'd just stepped out of the shower in preparation for dinner with Nick when my doorbell chimed. Sighing, I tossed my hair towel on my bed, put on my slippers, and pulled on a robe as I walked to the door. When I peered through the sidelight onto the front porch, I saw Baby Kelsey clutching her pink handbag with both hands. She shifted back and forth.

"What on earth does she want?" I muttered. Maybe I did need a pet. A dog might be happy to listen to me talking to myself. "Lord, help me be kind." I opened the door. "Hey! How's it going?" I sounded disgustingly chipper, but it was too late to tone it down.

She stared at me. "You don't look upset."

Why did she feel the need to always pick a fight? "Why would I be upset?"

"Because I'm here."

Had she been hoping to upset me? I stepped aside. "Come in. It's not exactly warm out there."

She shook her head, and her dark hair swayed. "I can't stay. I have to get ready for work tonight."

"Does staying up all night bother you?" I asked. "I'd be a zombie, and patients wouldn't want me taking care of them."

"I'm used to it."

"So... How can I help?"

"Why do you assume I need help?" Her eyes flashed.

I tilted my head. "Because I can't think of another reason for you to visit." The words flew out before I could think.

Nice Georgia.

Her face crumpled. "Why did I bother?" She bolted off my porch and ran for her gray Jeep.

"Kelsey, wait!" I chased after her, trying to keep my slippers from falling off and securing my robe because the neighbors didn't need a peep show. I'd heard rumors about Old Man Smith and a pair of binoculars that had me thinking twice every time I ventured outside.

She wrenched open her door. "Don't you *ever* tell Evan I was here, understand?" She got in and started to slam the door, but I grabbed it.

"Are you sure I can't help?" The wind whipped my wet hair, chilling me.

She collapsed against the seat. "I blew it with Evan."

"At least you didn't shove the pie in his *face*."

"It's not funny." She moaned and buried her face in her hands. "I can't believe I lost it like that."

I couldn't either, but I managed to bite my tongue before I agreed. "You like to eat healthfully, but that whole incident was *not* about the pie."

She nodded. "I'm so insecure." She scrunched up her nose. "Ugh! Why am I telling *you* this?"

Everyone knew she was insecure, but it'd take a better detective than me to uncover the mystery of why she'd shown up here. But she had, so I'd better do my part. "You have a lot going for you. You're pretty. Talented. Smart."

"How do you know I'm smart?"

"Because you wouldn't be a nurse if you weren't."

The edges of her mouth turned upward—just a bit. "Thanks."

"Have you thought about talking to someone to help you figure out what's causing the insecurity?"

She rubbed the steering wheel with her thumb. "If I go to a shrink, Evan won't want me."

"Kelsey, he deals with hurting people all the time."

She stared at her lap. "He deals more with student schedules and standardized tests."

"Yeah, I've heard him complain about that. But he's trained to counsel people, and he's passionate about helping others." I took a deep breath. "If there's one thing I know about Evan, it's that he hates it when people deny a problem and refuse to get help for it."

Her eyes glistened. "Do you think he'd give me another chance?"

"If you're willing to figure out what's causing your insecurity, and really work on it, you might have a shot. But if you don't, then your relationship will never work—with Evan or anyone else."

She swiped tears with the back of her hand. "Thanks." She started the car. "But you haven't promised not to say anything about this to Evan."

No one could fault her memory.

"I promise." I shut her door, and as she drove away, I wondered if I'd ever have the courage to take my own advice.

CHAPTER FOURTEEN

On Monday night when Brandi, Ashley, and I had decided to ignore each other at Salvador's Italian Restaurant in Richardville, it'd seemed like a smart idea. Then on Tuesday, the host seated us at neighboring booths next to a three-tiered fountain. From my seat, I had a perfect view of Ashley and Brandi, who kept giggling like a couple of middle school girls.

Nick leaned forward and jabbed his thumb in the direction of Ashley and Brandi's table. "That woman with the curly hair was my eighth-grade social studies teacher."

Oh boy. "Is that weird?" I kept my tone as light as the instrumental music that played in the background.

"Nah. I don't think she recognizes me. I've slimmed down since middle school." He chuckled nervously. "I used to have a crush on her."

I fought a laugh. When I'd invited Brandi and Ashley, I'd only referred to him as Tara's cousin, Nick, so Brandi hadn't made the connection. To my relief, our spikey-haired waitress bustled over and plopped a basket of breadsticks on the table.

"Welcome to Salvador's. I'm Jamie, and I'll be taking care—"
She clamped her purple-y pink lips shut and glared at Nick.

His cheeks reddened, and he cleared his throat. "Hi, Jamie."

"You dump me for a blond bimbo, and all you have to say is, 'Hi, Jamie'?" She muttered something under her breath that probably wasn't fit to be heard. Surely, she didn't mean *I* was the blond bimbo.

"That's not how it happened, so stop revising our history." Nick's voice didn't hold a trace of anger, which was impressive in the face of this ambush.

"You shouldn't have come here," she hissed.

He poured some water from the carafe and took a sip. "Last I knew, you were at Grey's Bistro."

She glared at him. "I can't do this." She whirled around and stomped away.

"My ex."

"Wife?"

"Girlfriend."

"I'm sorry."

"Don't be. She made my life miserable."

I glanced over my shoulder. "We can go somewhere else." That would freak Brandi and Ashley out, but it was a natural thing to offer.

I looked to my left, and Ashley's eyes were wide.

"I'd like to see how this plays out." He grinned. "Plus, I'm not going to let her run me off."

Interesting that he cared about having the advantage. Had he told the truth about not knowing Jamie worked here? Salvador's had been his idea. Was he making a play to get her back?

A thin man appeared at our table. "I am Salvador. Please accept apology. Jamie is, ah, what you call, hothead? I will provide appetizer free. Dean will be waiter."

"Thank you," Nick and I said in unison.

Salvador bowed and walked away, and Dean approached. We placed our orders without incident, and Dean left.

"Let's get the business out of the way so we can enjoy dinner." Nick folded his hands and rested them on the table. "What's on your mind?"

I wanted to dive in and ask about his alibi, but that would be a terrible strategy. "Someone tried to make Tara's death look like an accident, and when that didn't work, that person set up my cousin J.T. because he was secretly seeing Tara." I rolled the silverware out of my napkin and arranged the fork, knife, and spoon on the table.

He leaned back. "Interesting theory, but Tara never mentioned J.T."

"Did she ever talk about a guy she'd nicknamed Sharkie?"

"No—and believe me, I'd remember if there was a chance she was going to kick Mike to the curb." His jaw clenched.

After Dean brought our drinks, I decided it was time to switch gears. I told him about the letter Tara wrote to me. "Do you have any idea what Tara was trying to figure out?"

Nick picked up his straw paper and squished it into a ball. "Mike could've been doing something illegal at his restaurant. The guy has a reputation of being tough to work for, but Tara always swore he was good to her."

I swirled the ice in my Coke as I remembered Haley being allowed to study. "Who told you about Mike's reputation?"

"Jamie. She worked at his restaurant about two years ago. Said he has a nasty temper. That's why she quit." He rolled the paper wad between his fingers.

I wasn't sure Jamie was the best source, but I had to admit, some of Mike's crass comments had rubbed me the wrong way. It wasn't stretch to picture him losing his cool. "Last time we talked, you told me about Mike's criminal history. Why do you think

Tara was so willing to give him a second chance?" I clutched the napkin in my lap.

"When Tara was a teenager," he lowered his voice, "she was into drugs."

I bit my lip. "I'm sorry to hear that. How long was she clean before she died?"

"At least five years. Being off drugs helped her get her life together, but it was the whole Jesus thing that made her different."

"Does Morgan Hopewood have a drug problem? She seemed strung out at Tara's funeral."

"Yep. Tara was trying to help her get into rehab, but I worried about Tara being sucked back into that life. Mike was too, so I guess that's one area where we could agree." He cleared his throat and fiddled with the parmesan cheese container.

Now or never. "I really hate to ask, but where were you the morning Tara died?"

Nick gaped at me as the waiter set the bruschetta on our table and walked away. "At work." His posture stiffened. "Our network crashed on Sunday, and I spent the whole night fixing it. I left at noon on Monday." He crossed his arms. "Feel free to call my boss and confirm it." There was no mistaking the challenge in his tone.

"I'm sorry."

"It's fine." His tone said otherwise, but he picked up a piece of bruschetta and took a bite, and I did the same. The fountain's trickling water mocked our silence.

"Do you have any hobbies?" I caught Ashley's eye, but then horror crept into her expression. She said something to Brandi, who turned casually after Ashley nodded. Brandi's eyes widened.

"Golf. And I just bought a boat. You?"

"Music." What had my friends seen? "And gardening,"

"What's your favorite thing to grow?"

"Green beans..." Then I identified what had upset my

126

friends.

Cal.

And he was passing my table with a skinny brunette who was *rocking* a pair of what had to be four-inch heels. If I tried to wear those shoes, I'd take a tumble worthy of a corny sitcom. Not to mention the added height would cause me to tower over ninety-five percent of the male population.

Cal didn't notice me and put his hand on the small of his date's back as she took a seat in the booth facing me.

Thank goodness Cal hadn't seen Nick. Now, if we could be out of here before he left or went to the restroom. I pulled my focus back to Nick. "Yeah, I grow lots of things in my garden. Zucchini, peppers, cucumbers, strawberries, tomatoes, even some flowers. My mom helps me with canning because I'm not good in the kitchen and never really have been."

"Uh-huh."

"Where do you go boating?" I glanced at Ashley, who mouthed the word, *restroom.*

"Mississinewa mostly."

"Cool." I nodded. "Excuse me for just a second."

"Sure."

I hightailed it to the ladies' room and waited while I examined the bottles of lotion sitting between the sinks and picked Harvest Moon to slather over my dry hands. A few minutes later, Ashley joined me. "Sorry, hon. Brandi and I were arguing about who should come in and who should guard our table. Are you okay?"

"Yep. Although I wonder if Cal had already planned this date before he cancelled ours." The girl was the least of my worries. At least, that's what I told myself.

"Don't jump to conclusions." Ashley picked up a bottle of pumpkin spice lotion and squirted a blob into her palm. "It could be his sister." She rubbed her hands together.

I snorted. "My brother would rather have his hand cut off than touch the small of my back."

"True." Ashley curled her upper lip. "Mine would rather be shot."

I leaned against the counter. "What do you want me to do? Go up to Cal and find out?"

"Why not?" she asked. "When we prove J.T. didn't kill Tara, then Cal will be able to see you again, so you need to keep your hat in the ring."

"If Cal sees me with Nick, he'll know I'm investigating since he heard me questioning him at Tara's funeral."

"Cal doesn't know that your funeral interrogation didn't blossom into a date with Nick." She waggled her eyebrows. "Keep Cal wondering. Two can play at this game."

"What if he's not on a date?"

"Then it's a win for you."

"What did Brandi say?"

"You're stalling." She pursed her lips.

"Answer me."

Ashley huffed. "We didn't talk about it, but I know how you both think. For as brash as you can be, Georgia Rae, when it comes to men, you can be a real cream puff. You need to toughen up and fight."

Cream puff? "Easy for you to say. Every time I meet a guy, he meets the love of his life, and it's never me. I'm their good luck charm, remember?"

She rolled her eyes. "Or you quit fighting because you're afraid of what might happen if you win."

"Whatever. You should've let Brandi come in," I muttered.

"Nope. You two think the same way, and it's time to stop." She pointed to the door. "Go out there, say hi to Cal, and go back to Nick and act like you're having the time of your life."

"But Cal's date is pretty," I whined. "He's probably going to marry her." I hated how easily the excuses were coming out.

"You're going to die an old maid. I just know it." She reached up, put her hands on my shoulders, and turned me toward the mirror. "Look at yourself. Gorgeous. I wouldn't be a friend if I didn't tell you that chick out there has nothing on you. Besides, he could be in the middle of the worst date ever. You don't have the facts!"

The door opened, and Brandi rushed in. "Your date left."

Well, that was a first, though I had it coming for asking about Nick's alibi. I'd certainly never pulled that stunt myself. I hadn't even asked a friend to call in the middle of the date to stage a rescue, and I could've—at least once or twice. "But we already ordered. Are you sure he didn't go to the restroom?" I whispered.

She shook her head, and her curls bounced. "He called the waiter over and told him to cancel the order because he had an emergency. He paid for your appetizer and drinks."

I gave a half-hearted shrug for my friends' benefit. I wasn't interested anyway, so as long as Cal didn't realize what was going on, it didn't matter.

Ashley smirked. "Well, your problem is solved. You can go say hello to Cal."

"I'll think about it. Let me work up my nerve." My friends exchanged doubt-filled glances, and on the way out to reclaim their table, I overheard Brandi ask Ashley what she'd meant by the problem being solved. I powdered my shiny nose, hung on to my clutch for dear life, and marched out into the dining room.

I picked up my Coke and the bruschetta from Nick's and my table before taking a seat with my friends and making sure to keep my back to Cal.

"Are they looking?" I asked.

"No." Ashley took a drink of water.

Dean the Waiter showed up with Brandi and Ashley's

entrees. Then he looked at me, and I could see his wheels turning.

"Yep. I was over there." I pointed at our abandoned booth.

His eyes twinkled as if he'd put together what had happened. "Can I get you anything?"

"Will you put my order of chicken manicotti back in? And bring their checks to me when it's time." I motioned toward my friends.

"Of course." He hurried away.

I held the plate of bruschetta out to my friends. "Help yourself. I'm not hungry."

Brandi put down her fork and studied me. "Georgia, Ashley's right. Go say hello to Cal."

Brandi was supposed to be my ally, and now she was abandoning me? "Hey, did you know that Nick is your former student?"

"Really? Wait—don't tell me his last name." She squeezed her eyes shut and then opened them in triumph. "Vogler. He was a good kid."

"You got it." I gave her a thumbs up.

"I wonder why he didn't say anything."

"You're stalling. Again." Ashley pointed her knife at me and then turned it on Brandi. "And you're getting played."

"I've got to work on being more subtle." I winked.

Ashley rolled her eyes. "Go."

"Fine." I took a deep breath and thought of what I'd told Kelsey earlier. I needed to deal with my own insecurities. "Do I look okay?"

"Perfect," Brandi said.

I got up and pondered Life Lesson #83: Never cave in to peer pressure.

"Hey, Cal!" Did I sound too perky? Probably.

"Georgia!" He cleared his throat.

I hitched my thumb over my shoulder. "I'm having dinner with some friends."

"Right. Uh, this is Lindsay."

She looked me up and down in a way that clearly communicated I should get lost as soon as possible, so I stuck out my hand and forced her to shake. "Nice to meet you. This is a great restaurant. Have you tried the bruschetta? It's magnificent. I had it for the first time tonight. I sure wish I could cook like that."

Her eyes narrowed, and Cal shifted.

Put a sock in it, Georgia. "And how do you know Cal?" I asked.

"His cousin Kelsey introduced us."

"Good for you." My voice sounded too squeaky to pass off as normal. A few cuss words pinged around in my head. Why couldn't I play it cool? I forced a smile and turned to Lindsay. "Enjoy your evening."

"You did what?" Brandi's eyes flashed.

Later that night, we'd come back to my house and Ashley had gone home since she had to be at work early the next day.

Brandi curled her fingers into a fist. "Georgia, why would you think it was a good idea to set me up with a guy who tried to make out with you in the middle of a live theater production?"

Stifling a sigh, I curled my feet up on the sectional sofa and gazed around my terribly outdated living room. Why hadn't Ashley been able to keep her mouth shut? "Jon has a ton of fantastic qualities. Plus, he felt bad about the kiss miss."

"Ugh." She scowled and launched a throw pillow from the other end of the sofa.

The pillow smacked my face, thanks to her years of playing and coaching softball. I deserved the hit, but she could've lobbed it more gently. I rubbed my stinging cheek. "I don't have to give him your number. I wanted to see if he'd be open to the possibility." I held the pillow up anticipating another throw because she had one more projectile at her disposal.

She gripped the other throw pillow. "Now I'm the closed-minded one?"

"I never said that." I needed to salvage this—fast. I got up, marched into the kitchen, yanked open the pantry door, and tossed a box of shortbread cookies at Brandi, who'd followed me.

She crossed her arms, and the box clattered onto the floor. "Shortbread won't fix this."

I picked it up, ducked back in the pantry, put the shortbread back on the shelf, and held out a package of chocolate sandwich cookies. "Will these?"

"Maybe." A flicker of amusement danced in her eyes as she took them.

"I've got nothing else but milk to offer." I held up my hands in surrender.

She snorted a laugh and ripped the container open. She stuffed a cookie in her mouth and pointed at the refrigerator.

I took the hint and poured a glass of milk, which she drained seconds after I handed it to her.

It was a good thing we didn't drink alcohol.

"You don't understand." Brandi sat at the table, took another cookie, and pointed at the milk.

"You're right." I refilled her glass and poured one for myself. "I don't know what it's like to be a widow. Or what it's like to wait a decade to find the love of my life only to have him taken away after a few years of happiness."

When tears filled her eyes, she ducked her head and traced her fingers on the wood grain of the table.

I was hitting too hard. "I *do* know what it's like to be lonely." I joined her at the table. "To feel like life is working out for

132

everyone but me. To wonder if I'll ever have a family of my own, or if I'll have to be the spinster aunt who spoils her nieces and nephews and hopes that someday they'll take care of me when I'm old because I won't have any children to do it."

Brandi swiped her eyes and dunked her cookie in the milk. "You think Jon could be the answer to my problems?"

"No. We need God for that." I fished a cookie from the package. "But Jon's a solid guy who might be a step in the right direction."

She finished her second round of milk and slammed the glass against the table. "Fine. Text him my number." She pointed at me. "But if this goes badly, it's your fault."

The next morning, I yawned, pulled my bathrobe closed, and hurried down my driveway to get the newspaper. Angry clouds hovered, blocking the rising sun, and my favorite weather guy had said we were set to get the first snowflakes of the season. Fall could stick around another few weeks as far as I was concerned.

As soon as I grabbed the paper out of the box, a black sedan pulled into my driveway. I glanced down at my flip-flops. I wouldn't be able to run very far if the boogeyman or a mafia boss had arrived to take me away.

The driver rolled down the window.

Kelsey—clad in her scrubs. Must be something important if she was stopping here before going home to sleep.

"Good morning." I gave myself a pat on the back for not saying—or doing—what I wanted in the moment. Considering I was not yet caffeinated, it was a major feat. "Where's your Jeep?"

"In for an oil change. This is my mom's car."

"What's going on?"

She bit her lower lip. "When Cal moved here, I gave him

Lindsay's number." Her blue eyes pleaded. "I had no idea he'd meet you when I did it. I'm sorry. I'm so mad at him for going out with her."

"Why?" I shoved my hand in my bathrobe pocket. "He can't date me since he's investigating J.T. Besides, I've been out with other guys lately."

She bit her lip. "You and Cal would be good together."

"Cal's a grown man. He can date whomever he wants." My sluggish brain was having trouble putting all the pieces together, but the cold air was starting to wake me up. "Wait—did he put you up to this?"

"No. He texted that his date didn't go well and that he ran into you. I took that as a hint that I should intervene."

I did a mental happy dance before suspicion cut in. What if she was trying to gather evidence to use against me?

"Did it bother you that he was out with Lindsay?"

"I didn't throw a party when I found out." I shook my head. "You don't have to apologize."

For this.

"There's another reason I stopped by."

Seriously? I forced a pleasant expression onto my face. "What can I do for you?"

"I know we talked about me seeing a counselor, but I have another idea that could benefit both of us." She rubbed her thumb against the steering wheel. "I'd like you to be my prayer partner."

Good grief. I surely hadn't heard her correctly, but her pleading expression indicated she was serious—or a seriously good actress playing a joke on me.

I wracked my brain and tried to dredge up a single instance when I would've displayed behavior that could possibly make this poor girl think I'd be a suitable prayer partner.

I opened my mouth to say no.

Say yes.

I grasped the terry cloth of my robe and held on for dear life. Was God really telling me to accept?

Yes.

But why? For a second I had a vision of my mailbox as a burning bush, and I fought the urge to giggle. But, I knew better than to burst out laughing and hurt this poor girl's feelings. "Okay?"

I couldn't quite keep the question out of my voice.

She clasped her hands. "Oh, thank you."

"Do you mind if I ask why me?"

"Not at all. See, this spring before I graduated college, a chapel speaker challenged us to find a prayer partner. I've been praying for the right person."

"Me?"

She nodded and stared at her lap. "When we first met, I was so intimidated. You had this cool farmhouse, you're gorgeous, and you're thriving. You have a heart for God—except for that one time in the church restroom, but I totally antagonized you. You're where I'd like to be in ten years."

"Single?" We might need to have a serious talk about that one. And that she thought my eighties throwback house was cool.

She shrugged. "I need to be happy with who I am before I can have a successful relationship."

More doubts and excuses ping-ponged in my brain. How could God be asking me to do something like this? Brandi would be far better equipped to handle this situation. I'd probably warp Kelsey for life.

Trust me.

I wrapped my arms around my waist. "I'm free tonight. How about you come over for...uh...popcorn and sparkling water?"

"I love popcorn."

Finally. Some common ground.

CHAPTER FIFTEEN

When I walked back into the house, my phone was ringing, and I grabbed it right before it went to voicemail.

"Georgia, this is Nick Vogler."

"What do you need?" I fought to keep my tone civil while I poured a cup of coffee into my Sammy the Squirrel mug.

"I want to apologize for running out on you last night. I shouldn't have gotten so offended about the alibi question."

"Apology accepted. No hard feelings."

"I want to make it up to you."

"You don't—" I dumped a generous amount of cream into the mug.

"I'm not expecting you to go out with me again. I just want to make sure Tara's killer is caught, and you seem like you really want to help. Would you like to look for clues at Tara's apartment while my mom and I are packing it up today?"

I froze with Sammy the Squirrel halfway to my mouth. "Absolutely. When?" I congratulated myself for keeping the glee out of my voice.

"We're starting in about an hour. I'll text you the address."

As soon as I disconnected with Nick, I remembered promising Brandi that I wouldn't run around by myself, so I gave her a call. Since she was on fall break, she agreed to join me at Tara's apartment. There was the added bonus that her presence might freak Nick out since he'd confessed to crushing on her.

I used the business card Nick had given me to call his boss and confirm that he had indeed been working the morning of Tara's murder.

While I drove through Brandi's winding subdivision, I began second-guessing my meeting that night with Kelsey. If Evan found out we were praying together, would he feel like I was taking her side over his?

As soon as I pulled into Brandi's driveway, she came out of her brick tri-level.

"Thanks for letting me tag along." She patted the cognac-colored hobo handbag that I'd helped her pick out last month. "I'm packing heat, by the way."

"I feel so much safer."

"You should. You need to get your own permit to carry." She fastened her seatbelt.

I despised handguns, and my hatred had multiplied after Daddy had been shot. "I'll keep you as my bodyguard." I pulled out of her driveway.

"I can't always be around. I'll go with you to buy a gun, and I'll even teach you how to use it."

Right now, that was the last thing I wanted to think about. I cleared my throat. "So, I had an interesting encounter this morning." I told her about Kelsey's request and how I felt like God wanted me to say yes.

"God sometimes asks us to do things that we think are strange."

I turned off Main Street onto Pearl and parallel parked between a red SUV and an orange hatchback. "What if I heard wrong?"

"Then God will use this situation for good." She hopped out of my truck. "Don't expect me to talk you out of this."

I grimaced and slammed the door. "Was it that obvious?"

"Yep." Brandi stopped on the sidewalk and pointed to the two-story Victorian house with a wraparound porch and a few stained-glass windows. "I've always liked this place. Did you know a doctor was murdered here in the early 1900s, and they never caught the killer?"

I shivered. "No." There sure was a lot of that going on around Wildcat Springs. Leave it to Brandi the history buff to bring up an eerie detail. "And you *like* the place?"

"Yes, but I didn't say I wanted to live here."

Someone had divided the house into apartments, and Tara's was on the second floor. "Nick's text said the entrance is in back." We walked around the house and found the stairs that led to the door that Nick swung open before I could knock.

"Hey, Georgia." His gaze landed on Brandi. "And Miss Stedman." Understanding dawned in his expression, and his cheeks tinged pink. "Come in."

"It's actually Hartfield, but you're allowed to call me Brandi." We entered the living room with gorgeous wood floors. They had already removed the furniture.

"Right." His tone made it clear that'd be too big a hurdle to jump.

"What're you up to now?" she asked.

"I work for the Wells Corporation. Network administrator." He stuffed his hands in his pockets.

"I wish you'd said something last night at Salvador's," she

said. "I always enjoy talking to former students, but you all change so much, it's hard for me to recognize you as adults—even though I remember you."

"My ex was waitressing there, and it was awkward..." He glanced at her left hand. Brandi had finally taken her wedding ring off last year.

Merciful heavens. Could life get any weirder?

He pointed to the kitchen where a woman with fuzzy gray hair and a rhinestone studded denim jacket puttered around the kitchen. "Anyway, that's my mom Sheri."

Sheri dropped a can opener in a box, turned, and waved. "Hello."

"Thanks for inviting me," I said. "I hope it's okay that I brought Brandi."

"That's quite all right. My son owes you after walking out on your date." She looked me up and down and then shot her son a dirty look before turning back to the drawer. "He's always been too easily offended. Not sure I'm ever gonna be a grandma," she muttered as she tossed a turkey baster into the box.

Nick rolled his eyes. "Anything in particular that you'd like to look for?"

I glanced around the apartment and thought about the note Tara had sent. "Did Tara have a desk?"

"It's in her bedroom. We haven't donated that furniture yet." He led us down the short hall and pointed into the room. A double bed with a patchwork quilt dominated the space.

Brandi examined the quilt. "This is gorgeous. Did Tara buy this, or did someone in your family make it?"

"It was our grandma's."

"Is she living?" I couldn't remember what the obituary had said.

"No. Died about ten years ago." He pointed at a cardboard box of photo albums resting next to the bed. "Those might be helpful, so feel free to take a look. I'll be packing up Tara's clothes for charity." He shook out a trash bag and opened a dresser drawer.

"I'll start with the desk," I said.

"How can I help?" Brandi asked.

"Look through those albums and see if there are recent pictures of Tara with friends. We probably don't need her childhood photos."

"What do you think you'll find?" She perched on the bed, reached for an album, and flipped through it.

"Honestly, I don't know. More people to talk to?" I turned toward the desk.

The first drawer contained pens, pencils, tape, sticky notes, and a few stray paper clips. The top drawer had checks and stationery that matched the note she sent me. The middle drawer held a folder of newspaper clippings. There were several copies of Tara's mother's obituary. Another newspaper clipping was an article about the opening of Mike's Sandwich Depot five years earlier.

"Nick, did Tara work at Mike's restaurant when it first opened?"

"Yep. That was her first job after she got clean." He set a stack of T-shirts on the dresser. "I understand why she wanted to give Mike a second chance. It's because he gave *her* a new start at life."

"That makes sense." Another scrap of newspaper was an article about the closing of Irresistible, a restaurant in Richardville. According to the date, the restaurant had shut down without warning two and a half years ago, and the owners couldn't be reached for comment.

"Did Tara ever work at Irresistible?"

"No, but Aunt Debbie—Tara's mom—was the head chef for years."

I used my phone to snap a picture of the article. There were some more clippings of engagement and wedding announcements of people I figured were Tara's friends. I took pictures in case I needed to speak with any of them. Then, I put the articles back in the folder and searched the last drawer that contained a box of colored pencils and adult coloring books.

"Did Tara keep a diary or journal?"

"No idea." Nick shook his head as he stuffed some socks into a trash bag. "If she did, the police probably took it as evidence, which reminds me, I need to call them. We've been searching high and low for the accordion folder where she kept her important papers. Mom and I need the stuff in it to settle Tara's estate."

"I found the recent pictures." Brandi held up an album. "It's the last one, too."

I sat next to her on the bed and flipped through the pages. There were several pictures of Tara and her mom at a family Christmas. Nick and Sheri appeared in several photos. Nick confirmed the other people were family members.

Then, there was a shot taken at a beach with Tara, Morgan Hopewood, and Kevin Doyle. Kevin stood between the girls, and he had his arm around them.

I slid the photo out of the album to see if the date was printed on the back. Two years ago in July. Hadn't Kevin implied he didn't know Morgan very well?

"Did Tara or Morgan ever date Kevin Doyle?"

Nick shook his head. "I don't think so. But Tara and I weren't close until after Aunt Debbie died last June, so I'm not sure." Sadness flickered in his gray eyes.

I turned to Brandi. "Did you have all three of them in school?"

"Yes, but not together. I had Kevin when I taught high school at Richardville. The girls were in my class at Wildcat Springs, along with Nick." She smiled at him, and he blushed.

I slid the photo back in the plastic covering and found a few more pictures of Tara and Morgan along with several blank pages.

Brandi pointed to the albums she'd stacked on the bed. "The rest of these are her childhood photos."

Nick nodded. "I'm betting the more recent pictures are on her laptop and phone, and the police have them. Nobody really prints pictures anymore." He pointed to the album stack. "Most of those are probably Aunt Debbie's doing."

"May I look in Tara's closet?" I asked.

Nick shrugged. "Go ahead. It's not like the police haven't been through every nook and cranny."

I slid the mirrored closet door open, which revealed her clothes and shoes. After poking around, I closed the door. "No luck."

"I know what you should look at." Nick motioned for me to follow, so I did. "Tara's cookbooks. She was always making notes in the margins about when she'd prepared the recipe or who loved it."

"Debbie did that too," Sheri said.

He pointed to the stack of books on the dinette set.

Brandi and I pulled out chairs, sat, and I selected the *Taste of Home* cookbook on the top of the stack. "I really need to learn how to cook."

Nick laughed as he sat. "Me too."

A few pages into the appetizers, it became apparent that Tara had inherited the cookbook from her mom because there were two sets of handwriting. I recognized Tara's printing from the note she'd sent me.

As Nick had indicated, page after page held notations of dates when Tara and her mom had prepared the dishes—and for whom.

I skimmed the pages for familiar names. In loopy cursive

Debbie had written Nick and Sheri next to several recipes. Debbie had entertained several men through the years, including Max Jenkins, the owner of Wildcat Springs Implement.

He certainly got around.

Ten years earlier, Debbie had cooked chicken potpie for Pam and Joe. That could be Pam Marconi because she'd told me she'd hired Tara to work at Eatable in part because she'd known Tara's mother for years. Was Joe her late husband?

A collection of Italian dishes proved to be popular with Mike Dunson, whose name appeared next to at least a dozen recipes. Tara had even cooked a few times for J.T. recently.

After skimming through the remaining pages, I snapped a few photos, closed the cookbook, stood, and faced Nick. "Thanks for letting us snoop."

"No problem."

That night, I paced in front of the piano in my living room while I waited for Kelsey to arrive. "God, what are you getting me into?"

He didn't answer. Glancing at my phone, I half hoped to see a text from Kelsey telling me she'd backed out.

No such luck.

The doorbell dinged.

Kelsey stood on my porch with a case of grapefruit-flavored sparkling water on her hip. "I wasn't sure you'd have any." She thrust the twelve-pack at me.

"Thanks." I'd actually bought an unflavored variety earlier that day.

I ushered her into the living room where a bowl of microwave popcorn—my specialty—waited on the coffee table. She sat on the couch and flipped her purple and green scarf back and forth between her fingers.

"How about some of that grapefruit water?"

"Perfect." More scarf flipping.

Willing my head not to shake, I went to the kitchen and prepared her glass. I took tap water for myself. Earlier that day I'd sampled my purchase and gagged on the stuff.

But I was here to serve Kelsey.

I placed the glass on the coffee table and sat on the opposite side of the sectional. "How would you like this to work? Besides praying, of course."

Her eyes widened. "I'm not sure."

I stifled a sigh. Nothing like flying by the seat of your pants. "Do you have something on your mind you want to talk about?"

Kelsey bit her lip. "I've messed things up with Evan."

There was the understatement of the decade. "Why do you think that happened?"

She grimaced, let go of the scarf, and folded her hands. "I've always felt like I'm not enough," she whispered.

For a few seconds, my own insecurities and fears played in my mind like a shaky, unfocused home video. The too tall, babbling, music nerd with a manly profession. "What would it take to be enough?" As soon as the question left my mouth, it resonated in my soul.

"I'm not sure." She stared at the fireplace.

"You're a Christian, right?" It seemed like a dumb inquiry since she'd been asking God for a prayer partner, but I wanted to be sure.

"Yeah. Since I was fourteen."

"Me too. I'm glad God got through my stubbornness at such a young age." I sipped water. "Maybe instead of focusing on if we— I mean, if you're enough, you should ask God to show you how to be the woman he wants you to be."

She lunged toward the popcorn, and then froze with her hand hovering over the bowl. "Does this have butter on it?"

"Nope. Just salt. All natural." I'd known better than to buy butter flavored, though I'd have chosen it for myself.

She grabbed a handful and started shoving pieces in her mouth. "I'm thinking too much about me." Her tone was matter-of-fact, without a hint of defensiveness. "I should start focusing on others." She took more popcorn.

"I should've put bowls out." I started to stand. "Let me—"

"No. I'm good." She motioned for me to sit, took the big bowl, and arranged it on her lap.

Another question popped in my mind. "Are you afraid to be alone?"

Her popcorn-filled claw froze next to her mouth. "Yes." She released a few kernels from her grip. "I've always had a boyfriend since I was fifteen. When I'd break up with one guy, another one would be there to take his place."

While I understood her fear of facing the world without companionship, having a man during college hadn't even been an option for me. As much as I'd wanted it, nothing had worked out. Her experiences were so far from mine that I didn't even have a response, so I decided to go a different direction. "Have you ever asked God what he wants you to do?"

"No. I figure if the guy is a Christian, then I'm free do to what I want—as long as I don't have sex before marriage."

"Call me crazy, but I think Christians ought to have a higher standard for dating than just not having sex before marriage." *God, I need some wisdom here.* For some reason, I thought of Brandi and how her response was always to pray out loud—a practice that I found awkward. But since God had brought it to mind and we'd agreed to be prayer partners, I figured that was my answer.

"We're going to pray about this. Right now." I said the words with more confidence than I felt and before I could talk myself out of it.

"Okay." She nodded and stuffed the rest of the popcorn in her mouth.

I'd expected her to balk, but instead, she wiped her hands on her jeans, scooted closer, grabbed my hands, and bowed her head. Okay, then. That Christian college must've prepared her.

She lifted her head. "Am I starting, or are you?"

"I will." I closed my eyes. What should I say? Every time my Bible study group met, I avoided praying for meals or requests so I didn't embarrass myself.

On the other hand, I shouldn't worry about humiliating myself in front of a woman who'd thrown a tantrum that'd ended with a perfectly good pie in the trash and whipped cream on her boyfriend's face.

Just do it.

"Lord, it's hard being single," I said.

My words surprised me. I should've started with something more reverent. What was that acronym? Didn't it start with an *A* for adoration? I'd already blown the whole praising God thing, so I charged ahead because I couldn't remember the next letter. "But we want to serve you and do your will. Show us how. Heal our hurts. Help us not to put men in the place where you belong in our lives. Help us be content in all circumstances. Give us wisdom." I squeezed her hand to let her know that was all I had in me.

"Jesus, you're amazing," Kelsey said. "You're our father, our helper, our friend, and we praise you for your goodness and mercy."

ACTS. The prayer acronym was ACTS, and she'd nailed the first part—adoration.

"Please forgive me for thinking the worst of Georgia—and

other people. Forgive me for not always representing you the way I should."

Confession, check.

"Thank you for bringing her into my life and that she agreed to be my prayer partner in spite of my craziness."

Thanksgiving, check.

"Help us to know what to do. Help me to know how to be single and for Georgia to know how to be in a relationship."

Supplication, ouch.

CHAPTER SIXTEEN

The next morning while I sipped coffee, I added details to the board in my dining room, as well as the pictures of the articles and the beach photo of Morgan Hopewood, Kevin Doyle, and Tara that I'd printed out to have a visual. Since I hadn't talked to Morgan, I opened my laptop and checked Eatable's website for the day's class schedule.

There were several openings in the Shore Frolic class that afternoon. Even though it was an intermediate class, and I needed a remedial class, I booked it because the schedule listed Morgan Hopewood as the instructor. I'd be on my own because Ashley was working, and Brandi was shopping with her mom.

Gazing again at the board, another idea came to mind. Had Pam Marconi owned Irresistible? Is that where she'd worked with Tara's mother? I opened my laptop, did a quick search and confirmed that she had. Still, I couldn't find any information on why the restaurant had shut down. I mentally sorted through everyone who might know the answer. One name came to mind, so I grabbed my purse and keys.

"Have you asked that handsome detective on a date yet?" Bobbi Sue handed me a large Illuminati Latte and then punched my loyalty card.

I looked over my shoulder and prayed the customers were as engrossed in work or conversation as they appeared to be. "I don't ask men on dates." Not only was it true, it was the simplest answer. She must not have heard about J.T. being questioned for Tara's murder, or she would've been lamenting that instead of my love life.

She returned my card and put her hands on her hips. "How's that working for you?"

"Fine." I lifted my chin. "I like to be pursued."

"Fair enough." She pointed to my latte. "By the way, I gave you a double shot since you look like you could use it."

I should've taken time to slather on more makeup. Apparently, covering my dark circles with concealer and putting on mascara wasn't enough.

Bobbi Sue leaned forward. "Rumor has it you've been on several dates lately. Must be quite a change after that dry spell. I'm glad to see you're not pining away for that guidance counselor any more. Nice guy, but not my pick for you."

Dry spell? Pining? *Her pick?* I closed my eyes. I had to change the subject before another customer interrupted or I dropped dead of humiliation. I glanced over my shoulder and confirmed no one was in line behind me. "Do you remember Irresistible in Richardville?"

"Sure do. The hubs and I used to go there every year for our anniversary. Shame the place went out of business."

"Why did it?"

"I don't know Pam Marconi well, but the rumor among folks in the restaurant biz was that it wasn't making money." Bobbi Sue shrugged. "I don't believe everything I hear. The place was always busy when we were there. Not to mention, Pam managed to open that cooking school. I've always figured she wanted a career change." She flicked me with the dishrag. "You ever thought about taking lessons? Men love a woman who can cook." She lowered her voice. "Not that I'm all about traditional gender roles, but truth is truth, and I didn't invent the world."

I grinned and toasted with my coffee cup. "Here's to a double shot of truth."

That afternoon when I arrived at Eatable, Pam Marconi greeted me at the door. "Welcome back. I'm so glad you returned for a class. You're Tara's friend, Georgia Winston, right?"

"Yes, ma'am."

She marked on her clipboard, adjusted her round frames, and handed me a paper nametag and permanent marker. "Fill that out and have a seat with the others. We're waiting on a few more people before Chef Morgan starts class."

"Great." I wrote my name and stuck the tag on my flowing, leopard-print blouse.

The door jingled, and when I turned, Cal was standing there.

Merciful heavens. Thankfully, I'd put on more makeup.

His expression was inscrutable, but I detected the slightest gleam in his eyes. "Hello there, *Miss* Winston."

So we were back to formalities. Good to know.

He turned to Pam. "Cal Perkins. I'm here for the Shore Frolic class."

"Excellent." She gave him a nametag and clasped her hands. "Georgia, stay here a moment. I need to speak with the two of you."

Cal and I exchanged glances, and then it hit me. If he was

here for the same reason I was, then he wasn't convinced that J.T. had killed Tara.

I'd better be Nice Georgia.

Pam slipped off her glasses and put them on her head. "This class works best for pairs, and since you both signed up as individuals, I was wondering if you wouldn't mind partnering up. I was going to ask you anyway, but now that I see that you know each other, that's even better." She looked back and forth between us.

"No problem." I said a silent prayer of thanks that the words came out with ten times the confidence that I felt, because how I'd manage to cook with the dimpled detective at my side was a mystery in itself.

"We'll have a great time." He winked and put on his nametag.

"Perfect." She motioned toward the people waiting in the demonstration area. "Please have a seat with the others, and Morgan will be with you in a bit."

"What brings you here?" I asked as we walked toward our classmates.

"My skills could use some help, and I've heard the classes are a blast. How about you?"

"I can use all the professional help I can get."

"That's very brave of you." He patted my shoulder. "Admitting the need for help is the first step."

I laughed and rolled my eyes. "In the kitchen, of course."

"Of course." He motioned for me to go ahead of him when we reached the half circle of chairs surrounding the demonstration area. "And that's the *only* reason you're here?"

I sat and decided ignoring his question was the best strategy. "My poor mom tried for years to get me interested—even made me do baking in 4-H one year. After we had thirty nasty versions of a pumpkin spice cookie that my brother said tasted the same, Mom finally realized it wasn't worth the hassle and let me show hogs and crops from then on. She hasn't made a pumpkin spice cookie since."

"It takes a special talent to turn people off a cookie for life."

I chuckled. "That's right. Microwave popcorn is my specialty." I gripped the edge of my chair. "I apologize in advance for any mistakes I might make. I'm hoping my lack of knowledge doesn't cause problems."

"Miss Winston, you could never be accused of having a lack of knowledge."

In spite of my flaming face, I forced a wannabe grin into a demure smile, and batted my eyes—just a little. "Thank you. Having all the facts is important when making decisions."

There was a lot of sugar mixed with the venom in my tone.

"Good afternoon, ladies and gentlemen. My name is Morgan, and I'm your instructor for today's class. We're going to be preparing coleslaw, fried cod, and blueberry cobbler. I'll begin with a demonstration, and then you'll have a chance to prepare your own meal."

She appeared alert, but her chef's coat hung on her as if she'd recently lost weight. Her flawless makeup hid any sign of flushed cheeks. She began with showing us how to make the blueberry cobbler because that needed to bake while we cooked the rest of our dinner. Then she demonstrated how to properly use a knife to cut the cabbage for the coleslaw, and since I didn't want to lose any fingers—especially with Cal watching—I paid close attention.

That didn't seem too difficult. Neither did the recipe for the dressing.

I studied the other people in our class. One pair of well-dressed women looked like they were having a mom's night out, and my guess proved right when one of them pulled out her phone, rolled her eyes, and embarked on a whispered tirade in which she disparaged her husband for not keeping their brood under control. A mother-daughter team took notes, but the married couples interested me most.

Both of them were in different stages of the relationship. The young married couple, each with tattoo-covered arms, sat holding hands, fingers entwined. The other tired-looking pair dressed in khakis stared at Morgan as if successfully preparing a piece of fish would rekindle the lost spark between them.

If I ever found the right guy, would we look like the Khaki Duo someday? Maybe a relationship wasn't worth the hassle. There were definite benefits to living life on my own. I could spend my money how I wanted. Set my own schedule. I didn't have to worry about cooking.

Cal nudged my arm. "Are you getting all this?"

Morgan dropped the pieces of fish into her fryer, and they sizzled.

"Most of it." What had Morgan done to the fish before she put it in the fryer? Hopefully, Cal hadn't been distracted by the other people in the room and would know what to do. I'd follow his lead. A few minutes later, after flipping the fish, Morgan removed it from the oil, placed it on a platter, and everyone applauded as if she'd saved the world.

"Now, each team should go to an empty station, and you'll find all the recipes, ingredients, and tools you need. I'll give you step-by-step reminders in case you forget what I showed you."

As we approached an empty kitchen, my eyes fell on the fryer. I leaned over and whispered in Cal's ear. "I'm not touching the fryer. It's safer that way."

"You run a combine, and you're afraid of a fryer?"

"It's illogical." I pointed to the cabbage and knife sitting on a cutting board. "But I'm not afraid of the knife, which you could say is the combine of the kitchen."

Cal laughed.

"Start mixing the dough for your cobbler," Morgan said.

I measured and dumped flour in a mixing bowl while Cal put butter in the microwave to melt. "So... do you have any suspects besides my cousin?"

He cocked an eyebrow. "I wondered how long it would take you to ask."

"Did my restraint disappoint you?" I added some sugar.

"You lasted about as long as I thought you would."

"I hate being predictable." I dumped blueberries into a pan.

"I'm just good at predicting." He took the butter out of the microwave, added it to the bowl, and began stirring. "But, yes. I'm looking at other angles and have spoken with other people. However, we haven't cleared J.T." He dropped dough over the blueberries. "And that's all I can say."

I shrugged. "Fair enough."

"I'm glad you agree, because someone doesn't want you nosing around." He slid the cobbler in the oven.

I began chopping cabbage and wondered how I was going to talk to Morgan. Unless Cal needed a restroom break, it wasn't looking good. Still, I took heart because my investigation had to be on the right track if we were showing up at the same place.

I finished chopping the vegetables and tossed them in a bowl. Cal drizzled the dressing over them. We did make a good team. Now, to tackle the fish.

"Go ahead and batter your cod," Morgan said as she walked by.

That I could do. I picked up a meat tenderizer from the container of tools and reared back to pound the life out the sucker when a hand clasped around my wrist. I turned and faced Morgan, whose eyes were gigantic.

She let go of my wrist. "Not that kind of battering." She pointed to a bowl of what looked like pancake mixture. Cal must've made the batter when I'd been chopping vegetables and plotting a way to talk to Morgan.

He laughed.

"Oh." My face burned. I should've listened to Morgan's demonstration instead of wondering what it would be like to be part of a married couple.

Morgan patted my shoulder and then walked away.

Cal held up a dripping piece of cod. "We've got this." He dropped the fish into the fryer.

As he put a second piece of fish in, his phone rang. He glanced at it. "I need to take this." He started moving toward the front of the room. "Hey, Morgan, you might want to supervise." He hitched his thumb toward me and winked.

Morgan hurried over and peered at the fish swimming in bubbling oil. "Looks like you're doing fine."

"Do you know why your friend Tara was trying to contact me for help?" I said the words before I could stop myself.

Morgan blinked, glanced at my nametag, and her eyes widened. "I can't talk about this right now," she whispered.

"Why?"

Panic flooded her eyes. "Pam said if we discussed Tara's murder at work, she'd fire us."

That seemed harsh for such a jovial lady. "Seriously? She's the one who told me I should talk to you."

"She must've changed her mind then. I need this job, and I've seen her fire people over less. She can get weird about her business."

Was Pam trying to hide something? "When can you talk about it?"

Morgan peeked over her shoulder. "I don't know." She pointed to the fish. "Go ahead and take that one out," she said at normal volume.

I removed the fish from the oil and placed it on a paper towel. "Would you be willing to meet me somewhere after class? I have some questions about Tara. I just want to make sure the person who killed her is brought to justice."

Across the room, Cal caught my eye and gave a wave that clearly communicated he knew what I was doing.

At the next station, the Khaki Duo bickered over whether or not their cod was done. "Excuse me. I need to intervene." Morgan darted away.

I pulled the other piece of cod out of the fryer as Cal walked up.

"Did you have a nice chat with Morgan?" He smirked.

"She didn't give me the insight I was hoping for." I forced myself not to clench my jaw—or my fists.

"Too bad." He shook his head. "Sometimes it takes an expert to find the right information."

CHAPTER SEVENTEEN

After we'd finished eating our cod and coleslaw, the cobbler was still taking its sweet old time to bake, so rather than endure awkward silence with Cal, I excused myself and went to the restroom. When I'd finished taking care of business, I hesitated in the hallway in front of the ladies' room door. I could be good, turn left, and go back out to the kitchens. Or, I could turn right and see what was at the end of the hall and around the corner. I might get an idea why Pam was acting weird, at least, according to Morgan.

I picked right.

Before turning the corner, I stopped and listened. When I heard nothing but the cooking noises and chatter coming from the main floor, I moved forward, sliding my feet against the tile floor so my heels wouldn't click.

A row of tall cabinets lined the hallway. Pulling my sleeve down over my hand, I opened one of the six sections. It held a purse and a coat, so I shut it quickly and moved on. Ahead of me, an exit beckoned, but on the right, was the office I assumed belonged to Pam. The open door gave me a perfect view.

A messy desk stood under a window with closed blinds. To the right of the desk was a full-year calendar with a different vegetable picture for each month. Predictably, October's was pumpkin. On the left, framed pictures of Pam and other chefs adorned the walls. In one photo, Pam stood with Tara's mother in front of Irresistible.

A spreadsheet lying on the desk caught my eye because it contained the words *Mike's Sandwich Depot*. I picked it up and studied the information. It was the assessed value of the restaurant. Why would Pam be checking that? Unless she was looking to buy his restaurant. What if he was selling because he was in financial trouble? His restaurant hadn't been very busy the evening I'd been there. Had that been what Tara was investigating?

I replaced the document on the desk and picked up a framed photo of Pam and a young woman. It was Haley, from Mike's Sandwich Depot. Though Haley's frame was slender, she shared Pam's round cheeks and pug nose. Haley must be Pam's daughter. Is that why Pam didn't like Mike Dunson?

I returned the frame and stepped out of the office. As I rounded the corner, the back door opened, and I darted down the hall, ducked into the restroom, and stood at the door until the footsteps clicked past. Though I wanted to pull out my phone and check real estate listings for Mike's Sandwich Depot, I'd better get back before Cal came looking for me.

When I returned to the kitchen, Pam was talking to the Tattooed Twosome as they ate their blueberry cobbler. My heart did a flip. A few more seconds and she would've caught me in her office.

Cal's forehead creased in concern. "Are you feeling okay? You were gone for a while."

For a second, the urge to fib and blame greasy fish tempted me, but I shoved it away. "I'm fine."

"Great." He grinned and pointed to the cobbler resting on the counter. "Because I couldn't eat this all by myself."

After class was over, I waited in my truck and watched as Cal stayed behind and talked to Morgan. Eatable's large storefront-style windows gave me a perfect view. Judging by Morgan's crossed arms and shaking head, I gathered he wasn't getting any more answers than I had.

I guess being an expert didn't matter after all.

I took my phone from my purse and looked for restaurant real estate listings. I used Richardville's zip code to narrow my search, but there was only an Arby's and an Applebee's for sale.

Had Mike made an offer to Pam before putting his property on the market because he was hoping to unload his business quickly? The building that housed his restaurant contained neat possibilities for an entrepreneur looking to expand.

Inside Eatable, Cal finished talking to Morgan and strolled to the door, so I started driving home. I was about halfway there when my phone rang. I pressed the phone button on the steering wheel. "Hello?"

"Georgia? This is Morgan from Eatable."

She must've found my number on my class registration. "Yes?"

"I need to talk to you. Can you meet me at Zoe's Place at eight?"

I pumped my fist. Maybe I could get her to tell me what Detective Perkins had talked to her about. "Absolutely."

"Thanks. See you then." She disconnected.

I pulled into a church parking lot, searched for Zoe's Place on my phone, and let the navigation system guide me to the bar, which was in the dinky town of Redburg, about fifteen miles west of Richardville.

I arrived a few minutes before eight, so I waited in the gravel lot and noted my surroundings. Redburg consisted of some run-down houses, a brick United Methodist church, a one-pump gas station, and Zoe's Place, which I guessed was a biker bar judging from the dozen or so motorcycles in the lot.

Feeling like a New York City fashion designer at a farm show, I strolled into the cement block building and tried to ignore the creepy stares from the men I passed on the way to the bar. Rock music blasted and vibrated the floor. In the corner, some guys in leather vests played pool while a couple of women in tight jeans tossed darts at a board. Cigarette smoke engulfed me.

The scruffy bartender looked me up and down. "What can I get you, sweetheart?" he yelled.

"Coke please." My voice sounded squeaky in spite of the shouting.

He smirked. "Sure you don't want something stronger?"

"I'm sure."

He filled a glass and slid it across the bar. "You meetin' someone?"

"Morgan Hopewood."

He nodded slowly as if my presence suddenly made perfect sense. "Back there." He pointed to a back corner where Morgan sat nursing a dark-colored drink.

I tossed a five on the counter and made my escape. The music wasn't quite as loud in the back corner. I slid into the cracked vinyl booth and rested my hands on the sticky table. "Thanks for meeting me."

"Did you know that guy you were cooking with is a detective?" She narrowed her eyes.

I decided the direct and honest approach would work best

with Morgan. "Yes. He thinks my cousin, J.T. Simms, killed Tara."

Morgan sighed. "No way J.T. killed Tara. He's a good dude," she said. "We hung out a time or two at Tara's place, and I could totally tell he had no clue Tara had a boyfriend. I was the only person in on Tara's little secret. I told her it wasn't Christian of her to be stringing Mike and J.T. along and that she was going to blow it with J.T." She sipped her drink.

"Did you ever threaten to tell J.T. and Mike?"

"Um, yeah. What kind of friend would I be if I wasn't trying to keep my friend honest?" Morgan picked a hangnail. Across the room, a couple of men cheered, and at the pool table, one guy high-fived his buddies. "But I never had the guts to follow through—until after she died. I couldn't let Mike go around thinking she was a saint."

"What did you think of Tara's new faith?"

"I suppose it was real, but I thought Christians didn't cheat on their boyfriends." She shook her head. "Not that I'm judge-y or anything like that, but Tara totally kept trying to convert me until I told her to stop or we couldn't be friends anymore." Morgan met my gaze. "I'm spiritual but not religious."

Good to know, except I wasn't giving a survey on beliefs. "How did Mike feel about Tara's faith?"

"Okay, I suppose. He was going to church with her." Morgan swished the ice in her glass. "He doesn't like me, so I never got his thoughts about the whole thing."

"Why doesn't he like you?"

"He thought I was a bad influence on Tara. But I wasn't. Besides, she was an independent woman who had the right to choose her own friends."

"Was Mike controlling?"

She folded her hands. "Protective is more like it." She downed the remains of her drink. "Detective Perkins asked me the same thing. And by the way, I only talked to him tonight because he's in law enforcement and all the customers were gone."

"Do you think Mike killed Tara?"

"You mean is he the most likely person to have figured out where she was hunting and went to confront her about J.T.? Yeah, the problem with that theory is I didn't tell Mike about J.T. until *after* Tara died. He was super shocked, and I'm not sure he believed me. No way did he fake his reaction."

As much as I hated to admit it, Mike was looking less guilty. "Could he have been doing something illegal that Tara found out about?"

"I don't know what. He wasn't into drugs. Wasn't into gambling." She shrugged. "Honestly, I have no clue."

"Is he trying to sell his restaurant because of financial trouble?"

"Not that I know of. In fact, Tara told me his business was growing."

Weird. Unless he was looking at going into business with Pam. "Did Tara have any other friends who were having a problem she wanted to help with?" I told Morgan about the letter.

"It could've been me because of my drug problem, but I'm trying to get clean." She studied her hands. "I had a setback after Tara died." Tears filled her eyes. "I don't have an alibi for the morning she was killed."

She swiped away the overflowing tears with the back of her hand, so I rummaged in my handbag, found a tissue, and handed it to her.

"Thanks."

While she dabbed her eyes, I thought about everything I'd learned. I wasn't convinced Morgan had a sufficient motive to murder Tara.

"Okay. Why did Pam ban her staff from talking about Tara?"

Morgan sniffed. "She didn't want any negative publicity."

That seemed cold, but Eatable was Pam's livelihood. "Earlier you said Pam fired somebody for a lesser offense. What was it?"

Morgan rolled her eyes. "Us culinary instructors are never allowed to have our phones. One instructor got caught texting during a class, and Pam let him go."

That actually seemed like a worse offense than talking about Tara's death, but Morgan seemed genuinely intimidated by Pam. "Did Pam and Tara get along?"

"Yeah. Tara was Pam's favorite, which was totally okay with me because that's how I got my job. Tara put in a good word for me. Pam and Tara went way back."

"Because of Tara's mom?"

"Right. She and Pam owned a restaurant together." She squinted, as if trying to remember. "Irresistible."

My research had never indicated that Deborah Fullerton had been an owner. "Why'd Irresistible go out of business?"

"No idea." She flicked her gaze toward the door.

I had one more line of questioning to pursue and had better get to it before she bolted. "How well do you know Kevin Doyle?" A fresh wave of cigarette smoke worked its way to our booth.

"Tara and I used to hang out with him some." She bit off the hangnail she'd been picking. "But I haven't seen him that much lately."

"Why not?"

She shrugged. "Sometimes people drift out of your life, and it's better if you let them." She couldn't quite meet my eyes.

"Were you ever romantically involved with Kevin?"

A brittle laugh escaped her throat. "Um, that would be a *no*."

"Because he had a thing for Tara?"

163

"Nope. They were just friends." She crossed her arms, as if daring me to ask for more detail.

"Would he have any reason to want to hurt her?"

"No." Her eyes told a different story. She opened her snake-print clutch, withdrew her keys, and stood. "I need to go, but good luck with your search."

She rushed out of the bar without looking back.

Morgan was open until I'd started asking about Kevin Doyle, which meant that I needed to dig deeper into Kevin's life. Could he have been the friend with the secret Tara was about to expose?

A guy across the bar made eye contact. *Time to get out of here.* While I was leaving, it might be smart to look busy. I stood up, scrolled through my phone, and hurried toward the exit while waiting for Mike Dunson to pick up. Maybe Tara had mentioned Kevin Doyle to him.

Mike's voicemail kicked on. "This is Georgia Winston, and I have a few more questions for you. I'd appreciate it if you could call me back." I left my number, disconnected, dropped my phone in my purse, and exited into fresh air. A damp wind bit through my wool coat, and the moonless night tightened around me as I strode to my truck.

A shiver crawled up my spine and made me aware I should've stopped at the ladies' room on the way out. I wouldn't be able to make it back to Wildcat Springs. Before I turned to go back into Zoe's, I reached into my pocket and clicked the remote starter on my truck to warm it up.

Boom!

The force of the blast pushed me to the ground as my truck ignited.

CHAPTER EIGHTEEN

I lay frozen on the ground watching my truck burn. Waves of heat chased away the chill that moments earlier had penetrated my coat. My heart thudded as it sank in that I'd nearly met my maker.

Patrons rushed out of the bar, and a man and woman knelt beside me. "Are you okay, miss?" the woman with bleach blond hair asked.

I inspected my hands that'd broken my fall. A few pieces of asphalt were imbedded in my palm, but physically I'd be fine. I held up my hands. "Just a few scrapes."

"I called 911," the burly man said.

"Is anyone hurt?" I surveyed the parking lot, but other than the crowd gathered near the bar's door, no one was around. *Thank you, Lord.* I also said a prayer of thanks that I'd parked far enough away from the motorcycles that they remained unscathed.

The man and woman each took an arm and helped me inside the bar where they guided me to a bench near the door. The woman shooed the customers away. "Give 'er some space."

The patrons regrouped next to the window and door where they viewed the blaze outside.

"Thank you." A tremor erupted deep inside me and grew into full-blown shivering.

"I'm Dawna." She pointed to the burly man with a sleeve of tattoos adorning his arm. "That's my boyfriend, Frank." He stood guard in front of Dawna and me.

She rubbed my arm. "You're one lucky girl. Somebody must hate your guts. You a cop or politician or something?"

"F-farmer."

She gaped at me. "You growin' pot?"

"J-just your average Indiana g-grain farmer—c-corn and soybeans." Sirens interrupted our conversation and reminded me that I needed to call Cal. I should probably let Mom and Grandpa know too. I took a deep breath. "Excuse me. I n-need to make some phone calls."

Dawna joined Frank in guarding me while I fumbled in search of my phone that had worked its way to the depths of my purse. When I grasped it, my fingers still trembled, and it took all the concentration I had to pull up Cal's number and tap it.

He answered after two rings. "Detective Perkins."

"It's Georgia. Someone t-tried to kill me with a—" A sob choked the life out of my words. "A bomb. In my truck." I wanted to say more, but for once in my life, the words wouldn't come.

"Where are you?"

"Zoe's Place—in R-Redburg."

"I'm on my way."

Dawna and Frank wished me well and left their post once the paramedics arrived and looked me over. They cleaned and bandaged the wounds on my hands and suggested I get checked

166

out at the hospital, but I refused. Medical care cost entirely too much to go to the hospital as a precaution. If I had pain later, I'd pursue it.

A sheriff's deputy took my statement, and we were finishing when Cal burst into the bar, showed the other cop his badge, and told him I was part of an ongoing investigation in Richard County.

"I have everything I need." The deputy surveyed me. "You be careful out there."

"Thank you, sir."

He nodded at Cal, who sat on the bench next to me. Concern blazed in his eyes. "Are you okay?" He took my bandaged hands and examined them.

"Physically, yes. Emotionally? I'm pretty shaken up." Cal gave off a vibe that it was okay to be honest, and I didn't have to pretend I was tougher than I actually was. It was as if he had enough strength for both of us.

But that didn't matter right now.

He let go of my hands. "What were you doing here? I never pegged you as the type who hangs out in biker bars."

I told him Morgan had asked to meet me here and that I'd asked her some questions about Mike Dunson, Pam Marconi, and Kevin Doyle.

He sighed. "How'd she act?"

"Sad about her best friend's death. Until I asked her about Kevin. Then she was clearly hiding something."

He nodded, and his expression made it obvious there was something he wasn't saying—or couldn't say.

"What if Morgan is working with Kevin and lured me here on purpose?" I remembered what Susan at Fitness Universe had told me about Kevin. "He worked with explosives in the army."

"It's worth checking out. Did you tell anyone else that you were taking cooking lessons at Eatable?"

"No."

"Let me see the number Morgan sent the text message from."

I handed Cal my phone, and he made a note. "Is there security camera footage of the parking lot?" I asked.

"Nope. I talked to the detective in charge, and he said no one witnessed any suspicious activity around your truck."

"Or they're not saying anything." I glanced around the bar. "I'm not exactly one of them."

"Yeah." He met my eyes. "I'm sorry this is happening to you."

"Me too."

"If I told you that we have other suspects besides your cousin, would you stop nosing around?"

"Yes." I wrapped my arms around my waist. "But I can't make any promises if you go and arrest him."

"I'll give you a ride home." He stood and offered me his hand.

I grasped it. "Thanks." My phone buzzed, and I glanced at the display. Mike Dunson. Letting go of Cal's hand, I motioned toward my phone. "I need to get this."

Curiosity crept into his expression, but he stepped outside and began talking with one of the volunteer fireman.

"Hey, Mike."

"Whaddya want to know?"

"Did Tara ever talk about Kevin Doyle?"

"Yeah. The guy used to be her drug dealer. Guess he didn't learn anything after that other-than-honorable discharge from the army."

I hadn't seen that one coming. "Why'd he get discharged?"

"DUI and other stuff."

Wow. "Was he selling to Morgan?"

"Probably."

That would explain Morgan's comment about letting someone leave your life. "Why did Tara choose to work out at the same gym as Kevin?"

"You ain't the only one who wondered about that. I asked her point blank, and she said she wanted to tell him about Jesus. I told her to let someone else do that, but she didn't listen."

"Did you ever mention this to Detective Perkins?"

"Sure did."

I squeezed the bridge of my nose. What if Tara had threatened to report Kevin to law enforcement? "One more thing. Has Pam Marconi ever expressed interest in buying your restaurant?"

"No. But I did hear a rumor from one of my suppliers that she's looking to start a new restaurant. Guess that cooking school of hers is turning quite the profit." He chuckled. "Most days at my place are good, but on a slow one, I might let her make me an offer I can't refuse."

"Thanks for your time." I disconnected, stared at my phone, and tried to process the facts swimming in my brain.

"Kels tells me you're her prayer partner. How'd that happen?" Cal said as he drove me home.

First, I'd called Mom and then Grandpa, and it had taken me half of the trip to convince them I was okay.

I appreciated Cal's effort to distract me from my near-death experience with the other drama in my life. "She asked, and God urged me to say yes."

He glanced in the rearview mirror, made a lane change, and merged onto the highway. "God's funny, isn't he? Putting us in positions we'd never choose for ourselves."

"True." I decided to take advantage of this opening to get to know him better. "Has he done that to you?"

He kneaded the steering wheel. "Did Aunt Bev tell you I used to pitch for the Rangers?"

"Yeah. That's cool, by the way."

"Thanks. First season was great. Money was even better. Then my elbow gave out on me during my second season, and I had to have Tommy John surgery." He shook his head. "Never got back to where I was, and the team released me."

"I'm sorry."

"Don't be. The whole situation drove me back to my faith, and God led me into law enforcement."

"I'm glad he led you to Wildcat Springs."

"Me too." He smiled, but it didn't reach his eyes.

I sat motionless and decided it was a good time for a subject change before I burst into tears thinking about my rotten luck with men. "Will I see you back at church this week?"

He tapped his thumb on the steering wheel. "Maybe. I'm still looking."

"What are you hoping to find?"

"A church with reverence and respect for God."

"Really?"

"Yeah. A lot of services are so focused on making people feel good that they forget why they're there in the first place, which is to worship God and encourage one another."

"You don't like contemporary music?" I asked.

"It's not the music. It's the attitude people have when they approach God. He's not a cool beer-drinking uncle who'll wink at your sin."

I'd never thought of it that way.

"If churches don't take sin seriously, then people won't see a need for the gospel. We're misleading them."

"And you think my church doesn't take sin seriously?" I worked to keep defensiveness from my tone—not because I was upset, but because I didn't want him to think he was offending me. Truthfully, I wasn't sure how I felt.

"Not necessarily." He cleared his throat. "I'm weighing my options."

I'd grown up in that church, but it wasn't the church I'd grown up in anymore. "Where else have you visited?"

"Liberty Christian Church. I liked it. Felt like home. Solid biblical teaching. Music was a blend of hymns and contemporary. I'll give it a few more tries, but it might be where I land."

"I miss hymns." The music nerd in me loved four-part harmony and the lyrics of the old gems.

"Me too." Cal whistled "Great is Thy Faithfulness" as he turned off the highway and onto the road that led to my farm.

"My daddy used to whistle," I whispered.

I'd have given anything to have him here to protect me. Tears pricked my eyes, and my nose burned. I gazed out at the distant wind turbines with their red lights blinking in unison. I thanked the Lord every day that we'd stopped their encroachment onto our farmland because they'd sure come close.

"I haven't forgotten his case." Cal pulled into my driveway.

"I know."

I met his gaze and wished he could be more than a diligent public servant doing his job to protect me.

He shut off his car. "I'm coming in to make sure everything's okay."

"Right. Grandpa should be here in a little bit, and I'm willing to bet that my mom will show up." I got out of the car and closed the door. "My stepdad too, because he won't let Mom come alone if he thinks we're in danger." The circus would arrive at any moment. Not to mention, I needed to tell Brandi and Ashley.

"Good. You shouldn't stay here alone tonight."

"Let's see if the boogeyman's been here." I unlocked the back door, and Cal motioned for me to step aside while he walked forward with his gun.

Maybe I didn't hate guns as much as I thought.

"Stay behind me," he said.

171

I followed him as he checked each room of my house, which took a while since there were a lot of nooks and crannies.

Finally, he deemed the house safe and moved back down-stairs—and right into my dining room. Cal holstered his gun and studied the chalkboard with my notes and clippings. "Why is there a Pomeranian?"

"Her name's Polly. My friend Ashley drew her because she wants me to get a dog."

"A Pomeranian?" He chuckled.

"Doesn't seem to suit me, does it?"

"You need a guard dog, not a lap dog." He stepped closer to the wall. "I'm impressed."

"With the Pomeranian or the facts I've gathered?"

"The Pomeranian." He smirked.

I stuck out my tongue.

"You've certainly been busy, but you can take this down." He tapped Mike Dunson's picture. "He alibied out."

"Care to share details?" I removed the picture and crumpled it into a ball.

He cocked an eyebrow. "He spent Sunday night until Monday mid-morning with one of the waitresses who works for him."

"Which one?"

"Haley Marconi." Cal pulled the thumbtack out of Tara, Kevin, and Morgan's beach photo. "Where'd you get this?"

"Tara's cousin Nick invited me over when he and his mom were clearing out Tara's apartment."

"I see."

I pointed to the pictures of the articles. "That's where I found these articles as well."

"Good work." He tacked the picture back up. "Any idea when that picture was taken?"

"Two years ago." I leaned against a chair and decided not to take Mike Dunson at his word. "Are you aware Kevin Doyle used to deal drugs to Tara and that he got an other-than-honorable discharge from the army?"

"Yep." Cal crossed his arms and stared at the board. "I'm going to find out where he was tonight."

My doorbell chimed, and I started for the foyer, but Cal stepped in front of me. "I'll get it."

I peered through the sidelights. "It's Grandpa and his girl-friend Wanda."

They smothered me in hugs as soon as Cal opened the door.

"Georgia Rae, your guardian angel put his wing down tonight," Grandpa said.

"I used one of my nine lives for sure." Praise the Lord I'd had to go to the bathroom—and that I'd not wet myself during the blast.

Wanda rubbed my arm. "You look tired, sweetheart. Let's get you to bed." Her short, asymmetrical haircut gave her a youthful appearance. She faced Cal. "I don't believe we've met."

"Detective Cal Perkins." He held out his hand and shook Wanda's.

"Wanda Morris." She grinned and giggled. "I'll bet you're taking good care of Georgia." Wow. Cal even made seventy-some-thing women act like teenagers.

"I'm trying."

He caught my eye, and with my gaze, I dared him to keep talking, but he turned to Grandpa. "Are you staying with her tonight?"

"Sure are. Suitcases are in the car."

"Good." Cal said. "She needs a security system and should consider temporarily moving in with friends or family."

"I'm right here." I put my hands on my hips. "Some psycho isn't going to drive me out of my home."

"Georgia Rae, this person threatened you and then made

good on it," Grandpa said. "What do you think the psycho will do when he figures out you didn't die in the bomb?"

My head was beginning to throb. "Let's talk about this in the morning." I motioned toward the kitchen. "If you'd like some coffee, feel free to start a pot. I'd like a minute with Detective Perkins." I wanted to thank him for being here for me.

Grandpa and Wanda went into the kitchen, and my doorbell rang again.

I checked through the sidelight. Mom and Dan. If Cal hadn't been standing in the foyer with me, I would've muttered a few good, old-fashioned cuss words under my breath. Instead, I opened the door. "It's a party!"

Without smiling, Mom pulled me into a hug while Dan introduced himself to Cal.

"You didn't need to make the trip," I said. "Grandpa and Wanda are here."

Tears filled Mom's eyes. "My baby almost died." She choked me in another hug. "Dan's already left a message with the company that put in our security system, so they'd better call back first thing tomorrow."

"Excellent," Cal said. "I was telling Mr. Winston that was my recommendation."

"And you are?" Mom's eyes narrowed.

"Detective Cal Perkins."

She nodded and surveyed him with a hostile gaze. "Jill Farthing."

Okay, so his good looks didn't affect every woman he met.

"You're the one who suspects my nephew." Mom crossed her arms. "J.T. is a wonderful Christian man who wouldn't harm anyone. He took wonderful care of my sister after she had a horrible car accident."

Dan put a hand on Mom's arm, but she shot him a dirty look, which was the first time I'd *ever* seen her act that way with him.

"Ma'am, your frustration is understandable," Cal said.

Mom's mouth drew into a thin line. "Thank you for helping my daughter." She motioned toward the door. "We'll take care of everything from here."

I started to protest, but Cal shook his head ever so slightly. "It's great Georgia has so many people who care about her. I'll be in touch."

"Thank you." I wanted to say more, but Mom was moving toward my dining room.

"Georgia Rae Winston! What is *this*?"

Busted.

CHAPTER NINETEEN

"What are you thinking? You're not a detective." Mom swore and yanked down the pictures. "Stop messing around and start protecting yourself." She wadded up the papers and hurled them on the floor. "I won't bury one of my children." She pointed at me. "Do you hear me, Georgia Rae? I won't!" She brushed tears from her cheek.

"Yes." Tears welled in my eyes. "I'm sorry. I was just trying to help J.T."

She swiped her teary hand across the board, obliterating the timeline and leaving behind a wet streak. Polly Pomeranian remained intact. Grandpa and Wanda stood in the hallway, coffee cups in hand, watching the drama unfold. Mom brushed her hands against her jeans to remove the chalk. "Is that the only reason?"

"What else is there?"

"Look me in the eye and tell me this has nothing to do with your guilt about not being able to solve your dad's case."

I crossed my arms and looked her in the eyes but couldn't form the words.

"That's what I thought." Her face twisted, and she turned away.

Dan pulled Mom into a hug, and she buried her face in his shoulder and sobbed. I reached over and put my arms around her.

"We should all get some rest," Dan said.

For once I was thankful for Dan's peacemaking tendencies, and my tired brain tried to process where everyone could sleep.

"I'll be fine on the couch." Grandpa pointed toward the living room.

"No, I have enough bedrooms. Wanda, you can have Dakota's old room," I said. "Mom and Dan, my old room. Grandpa, take the guest room across from Wanda."

As I trudged to my room, I realized I hadn't talked to my best friends yet. I closed my bedroom door and collapsed in the middle of my bed. If I closed my eyes for a few minutes, I'd find the energy to text.

I awoke with a gasp and sat up. Sunlight peeked around the edge of the blinds. Rolling over on top of my bedspread with a groan, I glanced at the clock. 9:43.

I ran my fingers through my hair and gazed at my rumpled blouse and blood-streaked jeans.

Voices filtered through the heating vents, and I caught a whiff of sausage. When I opened the blinds and looked in the back yard, I saw Dan standing next to my pond talking to a man who had to be from the security system company because they were pointing at the house.

I'd better have some say in this new system, or I'd end up imprisoned in a fortress with no way to escape. After I brushed my teeth and splashed water on my face, I pulled on a fresh pair of jeans and a sweatshirt and charged through my living room toward the kitchen. I froze next to my sofa and took in the scene.

Evan lounged at my table reading the sports section and sipping coffee like it was his domain. Wanda sat across from him tackling a crossword puzzle.

My mom turned from the stove with a skillet in hand, strolled over to the table, and slid an omelet onto Evan's plate, which also held a generous portion of sausage. She looked up. "Good morning, sweetie!"

Evan threw down the paper, jumped up, and hugged me. "I'm so glad you're okay. I came over as soon as I heard about the bomb on the news."

"I told him you were asleep, and he could have some breakfast while he waited." Mom put the skillet back on the stove and thrust a mug of coffee toward me. "Do you want an omelet?"

I blinked because my decaffeinated brain was having difficulty keeping up. "Yes, please." I plopped down at the table.

"How are you feeling?" Wanda put dropped her pen and looked me over.

"A little banged up but fine." I held up my scabby hand. "I fell asleep before I could text Brandi and Ashley."

"They both called me when they couldn't get you." Mom cracked an egg and dumped it into a mixing bowl. "I told them to check in later."

Why hadn't she sent Evan away and told *him* to talk to me later? I stifled a groan that I didn't want to have to explain. Because she wanted him for her son-in-law, that was why.

My coffee was too hot to guzzle, so I resorted to sipping, as if that could cure the weirdness of the last sixteen hours.

"Your grandpa and Dan are showing the man from the security system company around." Wanda picked up her pen and resumed her crossword.

"I noticed."

"Dan told him to put in the best that they have." Mom dumped the eggs in the skillet. "They can install it today, and we're paying for it."

Normally I wouldn't want to accept a gift that pricey, but with our less-than-stellar harvest and buying a new mower, I simply didn't have the extra money to put in the system myself.

"Good," Evan said. "We don't want anything to happen to you."

"Wait, I get a say in the type, right?"

Mom frowned. "It's like the one Dan and I have—easy to use."

"Fine." I wasn't going to win that battle, even if I hated the new system.

Evan rested his hand on mine. "When you're done eating, could we talk?"

Something in his tone startled me, and I pulled my hand away. "Sure."

He'd probably come to tell me that he'd rekindled his relationship with Kelsey, and that, once again, they were rock solid. Evan needed to work on his timing. Or it could be as simple as him wanting to know why I'd agreed to be Kelsey's prayer partner. Maybe he was afraid I'd try to turn her against him. Or share dirt on him, which I wouldn't.

Yeah, that made the most sense. If he didn't like it that Kelsey and I were praying together, he'd have to get over it, because God had told me to do it, and that was all the reason I needed.

Wanting to hide, I picked up the news section of the *Richard County Gazette* and perused the headlines. One short article caught my attention.

Drug Dealer Arrested at Fitness Universe
RICHARDVILLE – Richardville Police arrested 28-year-old Kevin Doyle on charges of dealing a controlled substance

at Fitness Universe. Police took Doyle into custody on Thursday night, and he's being held at the Richard County Jail.

"It's shocking," Fitness Universe manager Susan Thomason said. "We have minors who work out here, and it horrifies me to think of them being exposed to drugs."

Behind the cover of the newspaper, I closed my eyes and stifled a groan. So much for Kevin Doyle being the murderer. Mom brought over an omelet, and I folded the paper and tried to act pleasant.

When I was done eating, I insisted that Evan and I take a walk outside because there were too many people in my house who were ready and willing to eavesdrop. He didn't protest.

We headed out the side door and into the overcast, and down-right cold, morning. I marched across the driveway toward the pole barn that housed most of our farm equipment. Grandpa had a few tractors at his place. I guided Evan away from the house and out of sight.

"Are we hiding behind the barn like a couple of naughty kids?" Evan laughed.

"Are you suggesting we have a conversation with Mom and Wanda watching out the window?" I raised my eyebrows. "Don't try to tell me they're not."

"Good point."

"What's on your mind?" I pulled my gloves out of my coat pockets and slid them on.

"First, I think what you're doing for Kelsey is great."

I didn't know what to say. "I'm sure it'll benefit me as much as it does her." That sounded cheesy, but even I could hear the ring of truth. "And you don't have to worry. I've never said anything bad about you."

"I appreciate it, but that's not why I'm here." He took a deep breath. "I should just get right to it." Instead he ran his fingers through his hair. "But I don't know how to say this."

"Just talk." I leaned against the barn's metal siding.

"When I started dating Kelsey, it was like this immediate spark that turned into a raging fire. It was so intense that I lost part of myself."

I nodded. *Here we go...*

"She was all I could think about."

My gag reflex almost got the best of me—like when I tried to eat yogurt. "We know —trust me, our whole group knows."

"But that fire is gone."

"Well, sometimes relationships burn hot for a time and then flame out." I fidgeted with the edge of my coat pocket. "A slow flicker is probably better in the long run."

He straightened. "Exactly."

Was he ever going to get to the bottom line? "Evan, we've been through a lot. Say what needs to be said."

"Okay." He started to speak, but instead, he closed the gap between us and pulled me into a kiss.

CHAPTER TWENTY

My brain told me to yank away, but my lips betrayed me and responded as he deepened the kiss. The roar of a passing vehicle barely registered as he pushed me against the barn.

I pressed my hands against his chest and shoved him away. "Seriously?"

His eyes held longing that I'd wanted to see for a good three and a half years. "Georgia, I think I'm in love with you."

I stepped back. "You *think*? What the—?" I blinked. "What brought you to this conclusion?"

"When I heard that someone had tried to kill you, all I could think about was how I'd feel if I lost you. Besides, dating Kelsey made me realize I had what I'm looking for with you." He closed the gap between us and rested his hands on my arms.

Merciful heavens. This was too much to handle. Cal. Jon. Nick. Evan. Which brought to mind Life Lesson #79: Never, ever pray for a deluge of men. Why had I done that? It had to be one of the dumbest petitions I'd ever prayed.

Yet God had seen fit to answer. *Interesting.*

"Are you going to say anything?" Evan's expression reminded me of a little boy, and my heart softened because I knew what I had to say.

Winstons were all about integrity, and no matter how I'd felt about Kelsey in the past, I couldn't betray her—not when God had turned my mailbox into a burning bush and told me to be her prayer partner.

I took his hand. "Evan, it was so sweet of you to come here and tell me how you feel, and I confess that day in the combine, I lied."

"I knew it." A grin broke out on his face.

"I did have feelings for you."

"But you don't now?" His smile faded, and his shoulders dropped, as if he were trying to hold back his disappointment.

I sighed and thought of Cal. What would he say if he found out Evan had kissed me? "I'm not sure. I care about you and value our friendship. But I agreed to pray with Kelsey because I felt like the Lord wanted me to say yes when she asked."

He raised his eyebrows. "Really?"

"Yep. Do you think I would've said yes otherwise? Especially after the Pie Incident?"

"Good point."

"And since I've agreed to pray with Kelsey, us having a dating relationship is completely off the table—for now." I squeezed his hand. "Plus, you need to figure some things out about yourself, and I do too."

"I know you do."

"Thanks." I snorted. "How about we pray for God to show us his will and for things to work if they're meant to be."

"I can live with that." He smiled.

So could I. But after meeting Cal, I wasn't sure I wanted God's answer to be yes.

"Hey, J.T.," I said. "I was just about to give you a call." After Evan had left, I'd retreated to the safety of my bedroom because the circus had not packed up and left my farm.

"Are you okay? I heard about the bomb."

"Yeah." I swiped dust off my nightstand and brushed my hand against my jeans.

"Thank God," he murmured. "What's on your mind?"

"Did Tara ever talk about Kevin Doyle?"

"She mentioned working out with him at Fitness Universe, but that was it."

"Rats."

"This is going to sound callous, but I'm freaked out about not having an alibi for last night—even though I have no clue how to build a bomb."

I stared out the window at the three Pekin ducks swimming in formation on my pond. "I know you didn't blow up my truck."

"Detective Perkins won't believe that."

"Then I'll convince him."

"No way, cuz. You can't put yourself in more danger."

I squeezed the bridge of my nose. "And you can't go to jail for a crime you didn't commit. Have you talked to a lawyer?"

"Yeah. I'm going with Scott Clark in case this thing doesn't go away."

"Good." I chewed my lip. "At least let me give you the information I've gathered in case Scott needs it to build a defense. It might help."

"I'll pick it up after work."

"No. *Please* let me bring it to you," I whined. "I have to get out of my house." I told him about Mom, Dan, Grandpa, Wanda, and the security system installer. J.T. didn't need to know about Evan, but since the two of them were known to chitchat like a couple of girls, he'd probably find out soon enough.

He laughed. "I'll be at work 'til five."

Eight years ago, when I'd decided to take on farming, I'd purchased a truck but hadn't been able to bring myself to sell the Grand Prix I'd driven during college. Even though I'd traded trucks once, I held onto the silver coupe that had a good 150,000 miles on it. It didn't cost much to insure the old girl that I'd named Gretel, and when I wanted to feel a bit more feminine, I got Gretel out of my garage and used her to run errands in town. That happened less often because my truck's sound system synced with my phone, and that was awfully convenient.

I was thankful to not have to rely on a rental—or my mom—while I waited for a check from the insurance company. Timmy Kingsley over at Kingsley Brothers Insurance in Wildcat Springs had been flabbergasted when I'd called about my truck, but he'd promised to take care of me. We'd been pals since high school and had been each other's mercy date for the senior prom.

It turned out I didn't need an escape plan after all, since Mom and Dan were satisfied with the new security system. They'd given me a lesson and returned to Richardville in the early afternoon. Before leaving to take Wanda back to her house, Grandpa promised he'd return that night to check on me.

Once I was alone, I smoothed out the evidence Mom had wadded up and printed new pictures with notes for J.T. and put them in a file folder.

I arrived at Wildcat Springs Implement fifteen minutes later and found the showroom floor deserted. Several employees were clustered in an office, so I walked over and cleared my throat.

"Georgia!" Max Jenkins burst out of his office as if he were scrambling to make a play on the football field. The group of men in matching polo shirts gaped at me with expressions I couldn't quite read. "What can I do for you?" Max shoved his hand into his pocket and rattled some change.

I held up the file folder. "I need to see J.T."

"Oh, Georgia." Max paled. "I'm sorry to be the one to tell you this, but J.T.'s been arrested."

CHAPTER TWENTY-ONE

"**H**ow? They don't have enough evidence." I didn't actually expect Max to answer, but the words flew out before I could stop them. We moved toward the front of the showroom, away from Max's employees.

"I'm afraid they do." He stopped next to a zero-turn mower. "I was going over my business's books and realized I had some money missing." He mopped his forehead again. "I traced it back to J.T. I was going to fire him and not press charges, but I got to thinking about how the sheriff's department thought he was a suspect in that Fullerton's girl's murder. So, I called the detective who'd asked me some questions about your cousin and reported it. Detective Perkins and Detective Kimball came and poked around. Not long after, they took J.T. in." He lowered his voice. "I guess they even found some bomb-making materials in his work truck."

I closed my eyes momentarily. Now Cal had a motive for J.T. killing Tara. Cal probably believed Tara had learned about the stolen money and had planned to expose J.T. "How far back did the missing money go?"

"Months. A little here and there over time, but it added up." His lips flattened.

"Who else has access to the records?" I rested my hand on a mower's seat back, as if that could possibly support the weight that had landed on my shoulders.

"My accountant." Max shifted. "One more thing. The detectives got to looking at the history on J.T.'s office computer and found searches on how to make a murder look like a hunting accident."

My mind tried to process the information. What if Max was setting J.T. up? What if J.T. had learned something about his workplace and had told Tara? Would J.T. keep the information to himself to protect me? But one thought pressed into me so hard my breath caught.

J.T.'d already lied before. And though everything in me wanted to believe my cousin was innocent, maybe it was time to realize he wasn't.

When I got home, I secured myself inside my new fortress and baked the tuna-noodle casserole Mom had left in my refrigerator. While I waited for supper, I decided to reconstruct my murder board before I passed on the information. I put the papers back up and included the details I'd learned about J.T.

Spinning theories in the privacy of my own home wasn't the same as running around talking to suspects. If I found anything important, I vowed to call Cal.

Besides, in spite of my moment of doubt, I knew J.T. was innocent and needed me.

Just as I'd tacked up the last picture, my doorbell chimed. When I saw Brandi and Ashley standing on my porch, I disabled the security system. She shoved a foil-covered plate at me as she sailed through my front door. "I figured you'd need these."

I peeked under the foil. Peanut butter cookies. Perfect. "Thanks."

She hugged me. "I'm so glad you're okay."

Ashley entered and gave me a hug. "Me too."

Then Brandi shut the door and put her hands on her hips. "Now that we have that out of the way, you owe us an explanation. Why did you go to a biker bar by yourself?"

"No kidding, hon." Ashley narrowed her eyes. "I've been cool with your amateur sleuth adventure, but I'm with Brandi on this one. You promised."

I winced. Nothing like facing the wrath of your friends. "I'm sorry. I wasn't thinking, but the person who was after me probably would've gotten to my truck even if I hadn't been at Zoe's."

"You didn't have to make it so easy on them." Brandi crossed her arms.

Time for a subject change. "Have you heard J.T.'s been arrested?"

Brandi and Ashley exchanged wide-eyed glances, which was all the answer I needed.

"What are we going to do?" Ashley asked.

While I walked to my kitchen, I smothered a smile over her quick change in tone. I pointed at the board in the dining room as we passed. "My mom had a fit when she saw this stuff."

Brandi frowned. "Then what are you doing?"

"Thinking—that's all. I'm planning to give all this information to J.T.'s lawyer tomorrow." I raised the plate of cookies. "Milk anyone?"

"Yes." Brandi said as we entered the kitchen. "But only if you promise me you won't go running around trying to stop a killer— and actually mean it this time."

"I promise." I took three glasses out of my cabinet and began pouring milk. "Evan came to see me this morning." We sat at the table, and I slid a glass of milk to each of my friends.

"And?" Ashley took a cookie and nibbled the edge.

"He thinks he's in love with me."

Ashley dropped her cookie.

Brandi snorted and covered her mouth to keep from spraying milk. "Sorry." She set her glass on the table. "What about Kelsey?"

I relayed everything he'd told me and looked at Ashley. "I need your expertise on men." I took a bite of cookie, and the sugary peanut butter melted on my tongue.

Ashley picked crumbs off the table and brushed them onto a napkin. "Evan deserves credit for telling you how he feels." She drummed her perfect nails against the table. "But what about Cal?"

"Considering he arrested J.T., I'd say any hope of a relationship just got obliterated." I turned to Brandi. "Your thoughts?"

"You and Evan did the right thing by agreeing to pray about the situation." Brandi folded her napkin into a smaller square. "Do what God leads you to do. Neither one of our opinions matter because you're the one who has to live with the consequences of your decision."

I'd just finished a bowl of Cocoa Krispies the next morning when my phone buzzed with a text from Kelsey.

We need to talk. On my way.

So much for being invited over. I sighed and trudged to my room to get dressed. Why had God asked me to pray with her? I didn't have what it took to deal with drama. Since I didn't have any special plans for the day, I put on jeans and a sailboat-adorned hoodie that I'd purchased on a trip to Mackinac Island several years earlier.

About ten minutes later, my doorbell rang.

When I opened the door, Kelsey pushed me aside and strode into my foyer.

"May I take your coat?" Cold air breezed in before I could shut the door.

"No. This won't take long." She marched into my living room and stood with her arms crossed. Her expression made it clear this was no social call. "I heard something that I wanted to clear up." Her eyes flashed. "I need confirmation from you."

Uh-oh. "A phone call wouldn't have sufficed?"

"I needed to see your face."

"Facetime? Skype?" It'd never crossed my mind that we'd need to discuss boundaries when I'd agreed to be her prayer partner. It wasn't like I didn't have more important things to worry about at the moment. I shoved my hands in the front pocket of my sweatshirt.

She huffed. "I need to see your body language."

I'd have been willing to step back from the camera to give her a full-body view. "What's on your mind?" I motioned toward the two wingback chairs near my piano. "Let's have a seat."

"Uh-uh."

I was starting to sympathize with Evan. When Kelsey was in a snit, there was clearly no reasoning with her.

"I totally trusted you." She put her hands on her hips.

"What have I done to break your trust?" I had a feeling about what she was going to say, but I had no intention of incriminating myself.

"You're trying to get Evan back." She shifted and reminded me of a snake ready to strike.

Play dumb. "What makes you think that?"

"You kissed him. Don't even try to deny it."

Aaannnddd, there it was. Did she have a spy network or something? I had a mental picture of Kelsey performing a dead drop at a bench in Sycamore Park, and a burst of laughter nearly spewed from my mouth. I stifled it and focused on choosing my words. "After someone tried to barbecue me, Evan came to see me yesterday morning. We talked, and he kissed me. I'm sorry."

"Did you kiss him back?" She yanked off her scarf and tossed it on my wingback chair.

"Yes. Sort of—before I pushed him away." I wrung my hands. "How'd you know?"

She wrestled out of her coat and threw it over her scarf. "My friend Brittany was driving by and saw you going at it by your pole barn." She put her hands on her hips. "Here's a tip for you—next time, remember people can see you from the road." Her face twisted and she took a menacing step toward me.

My face flamed, and I held up my hands in surrender. "It was just a kiss. Nothing else happened."

"Does he have feelings for you?"

How much should I say? I took a deep breath. Even though telling the truth would probably make Kelsey madder, that's what I had to do. "Yes, but I told Evan that I couldn't date him right now. It wouldn't be right. However, we did agree to pray for God to show us his will."

She looked at the floor. "I'm not sure I believe you."

"If I weren't telling you the truth, I'd already be dating Evan because for a couple of years, that's all I wanted."

"You're blaming me for keeping you apart?"

I put my hands on my head and clenched a wad of hair in my scalp. "No. I'm trusting God to provide the right man for me, and you should too. If God wants you with Evan, it'll work out. If he doesn't, he'll bring someone else into your life." I stopped myself from adding that God would also give her the grace to be single, but since I wasn't good at that particular grace myself, it wasn't a bright idea to dispense that wisdom nugget.

Kelsey dropped her arms to her side. "It hurts so much knowing I drove him away. He was different than the other guys I've dated."

No doubt that was true because, at the very least, he was probably more mature. I wanted to tell her I thought Evan's pursuit of me was likely a rebound situation, but I didn't dare give her false hope. "I'm sorry, but I'm not trying to steal your man."

"Evan isn't my man anymore." She sighed and dropped down on the chair. "What about Cal?"

"Nothing can happen with us since he's arrested J.T."

Her face fell. "Right. But what if that weren't the problem?"

"Then I'd like to get to know him better." *Because I'm falling for him.*

For a moment, she slumped in silence. Then she leaned forward. "We should pray."

I settled in the chair next to her. "You start." I'd learned my lesson last time.

After we both asked God for wisdom regarding our love lives and for J.T. to be cleared, we stood.

"I heard a rumor, and I'm wondering if it's true," Kelsey said.

I raised my eyebrows. "We shouldn't gossip."

"No, no." She swallowed. "This is about you, so we're safe."

Great.

"Are you investigating Tara Fullerton's death? Like a real detective?"

Of all the things she could've heard about me, this was one I didn't mind. "I was trying to prove J.T.'s not guilty."

"Was?" She tilted her head. "You can't quit now."

I motioned toward my dining room. "I have a board with some leads that I'm going to give to J.T.'s attorney. It might be useful as he's building a defense."

Her eyes lit. "No. Way. That's super awesome. Can I see? Pleeaase?"

I shrugged. "If it's that important to you. I need to take it down soon."

She grabbed her coat, followed me to the dining room, and pointed at the wall. "Awww. What a cute little Pomeranian!"

"Ashley drew it."

"Pomeranians and murders don't exactly go together."

"You're right. Polly Pomeranian is much too delicate for murder. A pit bull would be better."

Kelsey laughed.

"I should probably erase it..." But I didn't have the heart to get rid of Polly.

Her forehead crinkled as she examined the pictures and timeline.

"Well, now you've seen the murder board." I hoped she'd take the hint and skedaddle.

"Wait." She moved her finger along the timeline as if she was trying to figure something out. She unfastened Pam Marconi's picture and looked at it more closely. "This lady is Max Jenkins's girlfriend." She turned the picture toward me.

"Are you sure?"

"Positive. I was getting coffee Saturday afternoon at Latte Conspiracies, and they were there together."

"Do you know her?"

"No, but Max is a high school buddy of my dad's, so when I stopped to say hello, Max introduced this woman as his girl-friend." She grinned. "They made a super-cute couple." Her smile faded as she tacked the photo back up. "A few weeks ago, Max told my dad he'd moved in with his girlfriend, but they're hoping to get their own place once her daughter finishes her last semester of college and moves out."

My mind whirred. If Pam was dating Max, did that mean she

had access to the inner workings of Wildcat Springs Implement's finances and would've been able to set up J.T. and hack my yield monitor? Maybe, if she were tech savvy—J.T. had commented more than once that Max sure wasn't. What if Pam and Max were working together?

But why would either one of them have killed Tara?

CHAPTER TWENTY-TWO

A s soon as Kelsey left, I paced in front of my dining room table. I needed to get this information to J.T.'s lawyer as soon as possible, but I'd rather present him with a plausible alternate theory.

Mike Dunson had alibied out. Kevin Doyle had been arrested. Right now, Pam or Max seemed like the best suspects, but I couldn't put my finger on a motive for Max. If Pam killed Tara, then her motive could've had something to do with Eatable or Tara's mom, since they'd owned a restaurant together.

I should talk to Tara's aunt Sheri. Based on my impression of her when we'd met at Tara's apartment, she didn't seem like the type who'd mind if I asked a few more questions.

But my mom would have a meltdown if she knew I was investigating again, so instead of bugging Sheri, I called Cal. His phone rang and rang before the voicemail kicked on.

"Cal, I'd like to talk to you about some information I've uncovered relating to Tara's death, and it may prove that J.T. was set up. Please call me ASAP." I fought to keep my tone pleasant, but when I disconnected, I scowled and slammed my palm against the sideboard.

There was only one thing I could do. I'd head to the sheriff's department and hope Cal was there.

As I walked by my wingback chairs, I swiped up Kelsey's scarf that had fallen on the floor. I'd drop the scarf off at her house once I talked to Cal.

"Detective Perkins isn't here." A look of annoyance settled on the secretary's face, and she flipped her bangs out of her eyes.

Naughty words pinged through my brain, and I said a prayer of thanks that a thought bubble didn't float over my head. "Thank you."

She thrust a business card through the window. "Call his voicemail and leave a message if it's important."

"I've got his number."

She withdrew the card. "Then there's nothing else I can do for you."

I marched out to Gretel the Grand Prix, locked myself inside, and texted Nick Vogler.

> Will you please send me a number where I can reach your mom? I have some questions about your aunt Debbie.

In less than a minute he sent the number.

> We're at Mohr's if you want to join us.

I bit my lip. This was treading awfully close to running around tracking a killer, but it wouldn't hurt to go back to

Wildcat Springs and get some ice cream with friends in a public place. I texted back.

On my way.

I parked in the lot across from Mohr Ice Cream and Candy, which was wedged between Pizza Heaven and The Springs Antique Mall, and jogged across Pearl Street. The shop's black-and-white striped awning beckoned me inside, where a blast of warm, sugar-cone scented air hit my face.

A long counter with chrome stools upholstered in aqua vinyl made the place feel like a soda fountain of bygone years. Bins of colorful candy lined the wall to my left. Nick gave a friendly wave, and I joined him and his mom at their table in the corner. Apparently, we were the only ones in town in the mood for ice cream because the only other person in the shop was a teenage boy who lollygagged with his phone behind the counter.

"What can I get you?" Nick asked after we exchanged greetings. "My treat."

"Oh, you don't have to do that." I took off my coat and hung it on the back of my chair.

"Let him," Sheri said. "He still owes you."

"Well, if you insist." I grinned. "A small Mint Dream Shake, please."

"Coming right up." Nick hurried over to the counter and put the bored boy to work.

I folded my hands on the table. "Thanks for agreeing to talk to me."

"I want to know what happened to my niece." Sheri smoothed her fuzzy gray hair.

"I understand the need to have answers because my daddy was murdered nine years ago, and we still don't know who did it."

She shifted and fiddled with her sweater sleeve. "I remember that, but I hadn't made the connection that Ray was your father." She met my eyes and patted my hands.

I cleared my throat. "What can you tell me about Pam Marconi?"

Sheri fidgeted with the plastic spoon. "She and my sister owned a restaurant." Her tone broadcasted her displeasure.

"Was that a problem?"

"In my opinion, it was. Debbie thought Pam could walk on water." Sheri scraped the last traces of fudge from her empty ice cream container. "Debbie didn't see her own potential because she had such low self-esteem after bouncing from one man to another. Even though she was co-owner, she let Pam take the lead and make all the decisions, but my sister's food was the reason that restaurant was a success." Sheri's mouth flattened. "Abuse can change a person, and Debbie drew horrible men like flies. We never did know who Tara's father was. Not sure Debbie knew either."

My heart ached for Tara. How awful would it be to go through life never knowing your father? Still, if he'd been an abusive man, then Debbie had done her daughter a favor. I refocused my attention to the restaurant. "Why did Pam and Debbie sell Irresistible?"

Sheri shook her head. "I always hated that name—too sexual if you ask me. But it was Pam's idea, and Debbie went along with it."

Nick returned and handed me the bright green shake. "Thanks." I made quick work of the cherry that rested in a cloud of whipped cream.

"No problem." He took a seat next to me. "What'd I miss?" He looked back and forth between his mom and me.

"I was telling Georgia about Debbie. Anyway, I never got the whole story on why they sold—something about Pam wanting to take on a new venture—but it turned out just as well, I suppose, since Debbie got sick."

"How'd she die?"

"Breast cancer." Sheri gazed out the window at the cars streaming by. "I tell you. Debbie sure got a double whammy that year. Breast cancer and an early Alzheimer's diagnosis within a two-month period. Truth be told, it's probably good the cancer took her. Would've been awful for Tara to lose her mother to Alzheimer's." Tears welled in Sheri's eyes. "Guess it didn't matter in the end."

I put my shake on the table and focused all my attention on Sheri. "Was Debbie diagnosed with early Alzheimer's before or after Pam sold the restaurant?"

Sheri tilted her head and looked at Nick, who shrugged. "I'm not sure. Debbie kept things to herself and dealt with them privately, so who knows how long she was diagnosed before she told me." She emitted a tiny laugh. "She was seven months along before she told me she was pregnant with Tara."

I spooned out a bite of ice cream while I considered everything Sheri had told me. What if Pam had tricked Debbie into signing over her half of Irresistible? That would've been easy to do prior to her Alzheimer's diagnosis, especially since Pam already had power over Debbie. Had Tara suspected that's what'd happened when her inheritance wasn't as much as it should've been? "This is nosy, and I'm sorry, but did Tara inherit any money from her mom?"

"No need to apologize." Sheri shook her head. "Don't think there was much left since my sister had some debt."

"If we could ever find that accordion file of hers, we'd know for sure," Nick said.

Everything was starting to make sense, and I needed to talk to Cal. ASAP. "Thanks. You've been a big help." I stood and put on my coat. "One more thing before I go. How did Tara feel about Pam?"

Sheri's mouth twisted. "Like a second mother."

That would make Pam's betrayal all the more unbelievable and probably explained why Tara had wanted to investigate so quietly.

I grabbed my milkshake. "Thanks for the ice cream. I'll catch you later."

I raced out of the shop and tried calling Cal again when I was back in my car. This time I left a message. "Cal, I need you to call me or come see me as soon as possible. It's important."

When my eyes fell on Kelsey's scarf on the passenger's seat, I scowled and texted her to come pick it up. I had bigger problems than running a delivery service for lost items.

I disconnected and started Gretel Grand Prix while I wracked my brain for a way to prove that Pam had killed Tara. Fortunately, traffic was light because I was on autopilot as I navigated the roads out to my farm.

First, it was plausible that Pam could've found out that Tara had plans to hunt with J.T. He told me that they'd texted about hunting together. The cabinets where Eatable employees kept their coats and purses didn't contain locks, and their phones weren't allowed in the kitchens. Pam could've sneaked into Tara's purse while she was teaching.

Second, it was possible that a woman who may have cheated her best friend out of her half of ownership in a restaurant would be unscrupulous enough to access Max's books and change the records to implicate J.T. But would she have the expertise to hack a yield monitor? Unless Max was better with technology than he'd claimed and he'd helped.

Even though she may've known about Tara's plans to hunt, the thought of Pam sneaking out into the woods to kill Tara didn't make sense. Working around food meant Pam had plenty of easier opportunities to murder Tara if she felt her shady business dealings were about to be exposed.

Who else would've had access to Tara's phone at Eatable?

Haley.

Cal had told me Mike alibied out because Haley had slept over the night before Tara's death. What if Haley had lied? If she was starting a relationship with him, it would make sense that she'd want to protect him—and herself.

The night I'd met her, she'd been studying for a college chemistry test. Would she have the expertise to make a bomb and hack a yield monitor? I had to see if I could figure out her major.

Gravel popped under my car's tires as I turned into my driveway. My garage door creaked open, and I pulled Gretel inside, turned off the engine, and shut the garage door.

Not wanting to wait another second, I reached for my phone, opened Facebook, and located Haley's profile. A handful of recent pictures of Haley and Mike indicated she'd made their relationship public, but one detail made my stomach clench.

A student at Richardville Community College, Haley was studying chemistry and computer science and was planning to graduate in December.

My breath hitched. She could've hacked my yield monitor. Because if Max had moved in with Pam, and Haley lived with her mother, then Haley would've had access to Max's store keys —maybe even a laptop.

But why would Haley have been stalking Tara?

I froze as the answer hit me. To get proof that Tara was cheating on Mike, so she could have Mike for herself.

I slammed my car door and raced across my garage. On the way, I tossed my empty milkshake container in the can by the back door.

As I inserted my key into the deadbolt lock, a hand clasped over my mouth. A scream rose up, catching in my throat.

Thrusting my elbow backward, I nailed my assailant's bosom. She *oofed* and relaxed her grip.

I jerked away, whipped around, slapped the garage door opener on the wall, and sprinted toward my car.

Two more steps. I lunged for the door.

My head wrenched back when the attacker caught my braid.

I yelped and struggled while she pulled me into a choking grip. Cool metal jabbed my neck, and I glanced down.

A gun.

A sensation of a thousand spiders crawled over my body. The grinding whirr of the opening garage door stopped, magnifying the silence.

I turned as far as I could to get a look at her round face. "Haley?" My words were halting and raspy, and my pulse thrummed.

"I warned you to stop poking around." She narrowed her eyes.

"You're going to kill me like you did Tara." I had to get answers, and maybe I could distract her long enough to think of an escape plan. *Please let someone drive by and see us.*

"It'll be fun."

"You'd better hope it's more effective than the bomb you planted in my truck." *Seriously?* I wanted to shove the words back in. Forget Nice Georgia. If I wanted to live, I'd better be Smart Georgia.

A slow smile spread over Haley's face. "You got lucky. I'd been looking for the perfect opportunity to plant it. When I stopped to see my mom at Eatable, I overheard Morgan on the phone planning to meet you at that dive bar, and that was my chance."

Distract her. She clearly enjoyed talking. "The move with the yield monitor was brilliant. I'd never thought about them being able to be hacked, but why not? They're like any other computer.

Of course, that means there's the potential for things going wrong, but the data we've been able to generate through the years has been helpful. We're much more efficient than we—"

"Shut up!"

My talking-a-mile-a-minute strategy wasn't going to work. She pushed me out the back door and pointed me toward the grain bins that towered to the north of the pole barn. I dragged my feet, leaving trails in the rocks.

Haley tightened her chokehold. "Lift your feet."

My chest tightened, and I obeyed, which allowed her to steer me more easily. *Please, God. Let someone drive by.* I strained, praying for the swoosh of an approaching vehicle but heard only the metallic clang of the flagpole.

My ankle twisted, and I stumbled. Haley growled, straightened me, and pushed me until the pole barn hid us from the road. I glanced around, hoping Grandpa had left out a shovel or some tool I could use as a weapon, but, as usual, nothing was out of place.

An orange cat darted from behind the grain bins and took shelter in the old red barn where he resided with several of his feline friends.

She stopped at the foot of the southeast bin's spiral staircase that snaked up the side and led to the roof hatch. "Climb." She released her grip on my torso and shoved me forward.

No way. My stomach dropped. The platform at the top was thirty-three feet from the ground, which was why Grandpa and I had installed a staircase instead of a ladder. I faced her. "Why'd you kill Tara?"

She aimed the gun at my chest. "You haven't figured it out?"

"No."

"But you have a theory."

"Yep."

"Spill it." Haley called me a name that should never be used to describe a lady.

Dizziness swept over me, and I gripped the handrail to steady myself. The chilled metal bit my palm. "Fine." How long could I stretch this story out before she made me climb the stairs? I took a deep breath. "You're in love with Mike."

Haley's glare softened. "Yes. He's amazing." Her furrowed brow reappeared, and she waved the gun. "Go on."

"But Tara was seeing him, and he was serious about her. Then you heard she was cheating, so you started spying on her. You got into her phone while she was teaching at Eatable. You hoped to find text messages as proof, right?"

Haley's eyes darkened. "She'd erased all of her messages except the one J.T. had sent a few minutes before I looked. He gave her an address and said, 'See ya tomorrow. Can't wait to hunt.'"

"That was your chance to get evidence."

She scowled. "I had to find the place in the middle of nowhere. Figure out where to park my car so it wouldn't be suspicious. Hike through the woods." She wrinkled her nose.

"Wait. Where *did* you park your car?"

"The high school lot." She smirked, and her round cheeks no longer made her look innocent. "The Wildcat Trail goes right by the school, so I took it as far as it went and cut through the woods until I could see the tree stand. I hid behind an old sycamore tree to spy on them." Her eyes gleamed.

"Weren't you with Mike? You're each other's alibis."

"A little sedative in his beer, and he slept all night." She lifted her chin.

This chick was way too proud of herself. *Keep her talking.* "J.T. and Tara argued about her refusal to end her relationship with Mike."

"Yep. But I got lots of good pictures of them getting cozy before the fight."

"J.T. left, and then what happened?"

"Tara started sobbing. If there'd been a deer within ten miles, she'd have scared it off. When she climbed down, her foot slipped, and she fell. I thought I'd hear her yell for help—not that I planned to call 911—but she was quiet. I went over to see if she was dead. It'd be huge for me *and* my mom if Tara was out of the way." She waved the gun as if she needed to remind me who was in control. "Know why?"

"Because your mother tricked Debbie Fullerton into signing over her half of Irresistible before they closed the restaurant. Since they worked together, your mom noticed the changes in Debbie and guessed she had early onset Alzheimer's."

"Very good."

"Tara figured out what Pam had done when her inheritance wasn't as much as it should've been. That's why she was investigating your mom and why she wanted my help instead of going to the police."

Haley sneered. "Mom caught Tara coming out of her office. Tara made up some lame excuse that Mom pretended to buy, but she was on to her. We'd been trying to get a copy of her apartment key, so I could get in and see what she had on Mom, but Tara never left her keys in her locker at work. Always had them in her pants pocket."

Road noise caused me to hold my breath and pray for the crunch of tires against gravel, but the vehicle zoomed past. *Please, God. Let Cal get my message and come see me.*

Haley clenched her jaw and tightened her grip on the gun. "Mom thought Tara was so great. It made me sick. Growing up, it was Tara this, Tara that. At least until she was a druggie. Then she kicked the habit and went to culinary school, so Mom thought she was wonderful again."

"I'm sorry."

"No you're not." She waved her gun.

I had to get her refocused. A random detail I'd learned from Nick and Sheri popped into my head. "Did you take Tara's accordion file?"

"Tara may've been protective of her keys at work, but she gave me the perfect opportunity by leaving them in her car the day she was hunting. I used an app to take a picture of her house key and had a copy made. Then, Mom and I snuck into her apartment and grabbed the file the night after Tara died."

"Pretty slick, except for the part where you locked her car when you put the keys back in."

Haley's nostrils flared. "Shut up." She closed the gap between us and pressed the gun to my side.

I held up my hands in surrender as my heart thudded to my feet. "Let's back up. Something's still not clear."

"Go on."

"When you found Tara, she was alive, right?"

"She was unconscious. Shallow breathing, but I decided to put her out of her misery and save my mom and me some major headaches. So, I put on a glove, covered her nose and mouth, and got rid of a problem." She smirked. "Then I burned the camera and everything I was wearing."

"Smart. Except you didn't count on the suffocation showing up in the autopsy, so when it did, you had to have a suspect. You used your Mom's connection with Max Jenkins to set up J.T. With your background in computer science, it was easy."

"Max needs better security at that store. He's way too trusting." She wrinkled her nose. "He can't wait to have me out of my mom's house, so I didn't feel bad about messing with his stuff. Besides, he's always droning on and on about tractors. Total snore fest. The one time I was remotely interested is when he told me how much technology is used in modern farming and gave me a tour of the latest combine model. Anyway." She motioned toward the staircase. "Up you go."

I considered her possible plans. She could push me off the platform, let me splatter onto the ground, and play the suffocation card one more time—if necessary. Or she might be planning to force me into the bin where the corn would suffocate me.

Neither sounded like a good way to go.

I climbed three steps, whipped around, and knocked the gun from her grip. It clattered onto the gravel. Before I could jump over the handrail and retrieve the gun, Haley dove down, reclaimed the weapon, and aimed at me.

Boom!

I tumbled over the handrail, collapsed on the ground, and moaned as searing pain tore through my arm and stone bit my left side. Blood saturated my right coat sleeve, which now contained a gaping hole.

Haley slapped her gloved paw against my mouth and nose. Flailing my legs, I bit her hand. Darkness edged my vision.

No, please God.

A piercing scream sliced the air.

CHAPTER TWENTY-THREE

Haley lifted her hand from my nose and mouth as she whirled toward the scream. I gulped oxygen and lifted my head.

Kelsey stood with her hands up, her phone on the ground beside her.

My heart dropped.

Haley leveled the gun at Kelsey's chest. "Get over here."

Kelsey's jaw tightened, and for a split second it seemed like she was about to tell Haley no, but she stepped forward, her leopard print heels causing her to teeter in the rocks.

I couldn't let Kelsey die—not when this was all my fault. Pushing my left hand into the rocks, I forced myself to sit up on my left hip. Another wave of dizziness rolled through my vision. When it passed, Kelsey met my eyes. Though they were fear-filled, a grim resolve settled in her expression.

"I came to get my scarf," she said.

"You should've called first," Haley jeered.

Using my left hand for leverage, I stumbled to my feet.

Haley's face twisted as she swung toward me.

I met Kelsey's eyes again, and she lunged at Haley's abdomen as I leaped at her back.

"Ooofff." Haley doubled over as we sandwiched her—and because I outweighed Haley by a good fifty pounds. My fingers clawed her shoulders while Kelsey wrenched the gun from her hand and aimed it at her.

Haley swore.

Kelsey held the weapon steady while I pushed my knee in Haley's back, forcing her to the ground. Keeping my weight on her, I used my left hand to pull the string out of the hood on my sweatshirt. I held it out to Kelsey. "I can't use my right arm."

Her eyes clouded with concern as they fell on my blood-soaked arm. "Yep." She put the gun on the ground out of Haley's reach before using the string to bind her hands. I kept pressure on Haley's back as she bucked back and forth using cuss words as nouns, adjectives, and verbs.

When Haley's hands were secure, Kelsey scrambled to her phone, picked it up, and raced back toward me, dialing as she ran. "I'm calling 911."

The paramedic wheeled me toward the ambulance, amid the chaos that'd broken out on my farm. Sheriff's deputies swarmed around. Grandpa had gotten a call from Old Man Smith, who monitored the police scanner, and had arrived at the same time as the ambulance. He was sitting in his truck, waiting to follow the ambulance to Richard County Hospital.

Cal raced to my side and grasped my left hand. His blue eyes filled with concern.

"I'm sorry I didn't get your message sooner." He let go of my hand, and the paramedic loaded me into the ambulance.

"Haley killed Tara," I croaked. "She set up J.T."

"I'll take care of everything." He squeezed my hand. "Focus on getting better. You did great today."

I managed to catch a glimpse of Cal's dimple before the paramedic slammed the ambulance door.

It turned out the bullet had passed through my fleshy arm, leaving no permanent damage, a fact for which I thanked the good Lord. Between that and having the bulk to take down Haley, I guessed God knew what he was doing, giving me some extra meat on my bones.

In spite of my injury being a flesh wound, the ER doctor decided to bilk my insurance and keep me in the hospital overnight for observation. Even though Mom wanted to stay, I told her to go home and get the rest I wouldn't be getting.

The next morning, Kelsey arrived and hesitated at the door of my room. She clutched a vase of daisies.

"Hey! Come in."

She extended the flowers. "I hope you like daisies. I thought they were cheerful."

I took them. "They are. Thanks." I pointed to the chair at the foot of my bed. "Have a seat."

She perched on the edge as if she were afraid of getting too comfortable.

"Sorry you didn't get your scarf back yesterday."

She laughed. "Oh, Georgia."

But my humor had worked, and she relaxed.

"Seriously, though. Thank you. If we hadn't become prayer partners and you hadn't stopped by..."

She unzipped her black moto jacket, took it off, and set it

aside. "I'm glad you're okay. Cal's planning to drop by on his lunch break if you're still here."

I sighed. "The doctor told me this morning they're going to spring me, but we both know it'll take all day."

She laughed. "I wish I could tell you differently." She glanced out the window at the brick wall.

I fidgeted with the edge of my blanket. "Is something else on your mind?"

"Yeah." She fingered her silver cross necklace. "I'm going to the mission field for a year."

"Really?" I pressed the button on my bed and propped it up more. We hadn't prayed about that, so her announcement felt like it was coming out of nowhere. "Where?"

"Ethiopia. There's a clinic there that needs nurses. I didn't tell you about it because I was in denial."

"How so?"

She wrapped her arms around her waist. "God's been bugging me about serving overseas since before I graduated, but when I met Evan, I thought I'd heard God wrong—at least that's what I've been telling myself."

No wonder she'd been insecure about their relationship. Deep down, she'd known it wasn't what God wanted—for now. "Have you told Evan?"

"No. But if we're meant to be, it'll work out when I come home."

How would he respond if she never came home?

"That's great," I said. "Let me know if you need financial support. I'll do whatever I can."

"Thanks."

"Financial support for what?" Evan stood in the doorway with a box of chocolates, which I had the feeling I was going to need very soon.

Kelsey and I exchanged glances.

She stood and faced him. "I'm going to Ethiopia for a year to work in a clinic."

Evan laughed. "That's a good one."

"I'm serious." She lifted her chin.

He stared at her. "You're running away?"

"No." Peace radiated in her expression. "I've finally *stopped* running."

He swallowed hard, and his shoulders sagged. The silence in the room grew unbearable. If there had been a way for me to dive under the covers and teleport to any other room in the joint—including the morgue—I'd have done it.

I cleared my throat. "If you want to talk, there's a nice waiting room at the end of the hall—but leave the chocolate."

Kelsey nodded and picked up her jacket. "That's a good idea," she whispered.

Evan handed the box over with a rueful smile, and as I watched them go, I felt at peace about the answer I'd been seeking.

"I didn't see *that* coming," Evan said about twenty minutes later. While he'd powwowed with Kelsey, I'd entertained myself with *The Price Is Right* and made a serious dent in the chocolate caramels sprinkled with sea salt.

I shut off the TV. "How'd you and Kelsey leave things?"

"She promised to keep in touch." He shook his head and sat in the chair next to my bed, resting his hands on his thighs. "I've messed everything up."

"Not everything." I pointed to the chocolate box. "You did well with these."

"Thanks." He studied me as if he couldn't figure out what to say next.

"We're just supposed to be friends," I blurted.

"I know." He leaned back. "I was going to tell you I'd figured that out when you got out of here."

"Why wait?" The edge of my mouth twitched. "It's not going to affect my will to live."

He chuckled and raised his palms. "Never crossed my mind."

"You're bored, aren't you?" That afternoon, Cal strolled into my room holding a vase with a yellow rose. A smiley face balloon bobbed above it.

"Of course not. Hospital stays are thrilling. It's riveting seeing the different scrubs the nurses are wearing. One of my night nurses was a guy, and he had on Colts scrubs, which were my favorite."

He laughed.

"Thanks for the flower and balloon."

"You're welcome." He looked around, and an awkward silence settled over my room.

I'll nip that in the bud. "Have you released my cousin?" No sense in dancing around the major issue.

Cal set the vase on the shelf across from my bed and dragged a chair over to my bedside. "J.T.'s been exonerated, thanks to you." His tone and expression were free of resentment, but that seemed too good to be true. Didn't it bother him that he'd been wrong, and I'd been right?

Cal pulled a newspaper from his jacket and unfolded it so I could see the headline. "You made the front page."

Local Woman Arrested in Fullerton Murder

I wrinkled my nose as I skimmed the article. "I wish they'd

highlighted the fact that my sacrifice helped solve a murder instead of me ending up almost dying."

"Keep reading."

I skimmed until I found the mention of my information being used to solve Tara's murder. Then I put the paper in my lap and focused on Cal. "Now what?" I'd let him interpret that question however he wished.

"Haley gave a full confession, and we're investigating her mother for fraud."

We can talk about the case. I willed disappointment from my expression. "I'm glad." Nick and Sheri—and everyone who loved Tara—had the answers they deserved. If only my family were so lucky...

"The good news is, barring any upcoming crime sprees, I can focus on your dad's investigation now."

"That's great. Thanks." I ran my finger over the blanket's rough surface.

"When you get out of here, I'd like to talk about the research you did on his case." He cracked his knuckles. "We could even do that over dinner, if you're not still mad at me for arresting your cousin."

I twisted a wad of blanket. "You were doing your job." I met his eyes and wanted to forget the question that hovered. But I had to know. "Do you resent me for solving the case?"

"Fair question." He ran his hands through his hair and met my gaze. "But justice is more important than my pride, and I'm sorry I was wrong about J.T."

I reached for his hand and gave it a squeeze. "Then, yes. I'd love to have dinner with you."

Near-death experiences impact everybody differently. Some people vow to serve God. Some people buy a fancy sports car. Since I was already serving God and couldn't care less about a fancy set of wheels, my trauma influenced me to get a dog.

And I even agreed to talk to a counselor that Pastor Mark had recommended.

The day after I was released from the hospital, Brandi had driven me to a breeder's house in Indianapolis where I'd purchased an eight-week-old—housebroken—yellow Labrador retriever.

That night, the pup still didn't have a name, and Brandi, Ashley, and I sat on my living room floor while my dog-child bounded between us, nipping our fingers and charming us with his puppy antics.

"His paws are huge," Ashley said. "Are you sure you want him to be an inside dog? He's going to be massive when he's full grown."

I was quite aware of this fact, having met the dog's seventy-pound mother and eighty-five-pound father. "I thought you wanted me to have a pet."

"Hon, I strongly hinted for a Pomeranian, but no one ever listens to me. I just don't want you to be sorry when this cute little angel is the size of a small horse."

I covered the dog's ears. "Don't say that in front of him."

Brandi laughed. "I think you should name him Buddy."

I cocked an eyebrow. "He's supposed to be my guard dog."

"Beast?" Ashley said.

I picked up the dog and cuddled him. "How can you look at this face and suggest that he's a beast?"

"If you called him Beast, he might live up to the name instead of licking intruders to death." Ashley held out her hand, and the dog swiped it with his tongue.

I stroked the puppy's head. We'd think of something perfect soon. "Have you set up a date with Jon?"

Brandi crossed her arms. "As a matter of fact, I have. We're going out on Saturday."

"Yay!" Ashley clasped her hands. "Have you decided on your outfit? Do you want me to paint your nails?"

Brandi smiled. "No. And yes."

"What about Cal?" Ashley asked. "Tell me there's hope now that J.T.'s been cleared."

"Yes." I updated them on our last conversation.

"I'm glad he's not upset with you," Brandi said.

"And the Evan thing?" Ashley eyed me as if she weren't sure it could possibly be true that I was over him.

But it was. "God's given me peace about Evan and me being friends, and I've moved on." God would provide the right man for me. It might end up being Cal, or it could be someone else. God would show me in time.

"I thought of a name," Brandi said. "This is so perfect, I can't believe we didn't think of it sooner."

Oh boy.

She clasped her hands. "He's going to be your sidekick, right?"

"Yep."

She grinned. "Then how about Guster—Gus for short?"

I blinked. The name *was* perfect. Brandi knew me well.

Ashley squealed. "I love it."

"Well?" Brandi leaned forward and met my eyes.

I turned the dog to face me. "Do you want to be called Gus?"

He licked my face, and all three of us laughed.

"I guess that answers our question." I kissed his furry head. "Gus Winston it is."

Don't miss Georgia's next adventure in *Deadly Holiday*. If you want to be the first to know about new releases, sign up for my email newsletter at marissashrock.com. I won't share your email with anyone, and as a thank you for joining, you'll gain access to *Deadly Homestead: A Georgia Rae Winston Mini-Mystery and Other Short Stories.*

ABOUT THE AUTHOR

Jenni Mansell Photography

Marissa Shrock is a survivor of many awkward blind dates and many years of teaching middle school. Both provide excellent inspiration for her fictional yarns.

Since childhood, she's loved to read a variety of genres, so her own work includes dystopian thrillers and cozy mysteries. She's the author of the Emancipation Warriors Series and the Georgia Rae Winston Mystery Series. Her debut novel, *The First Principle*, was a Carol Award Finalist.

Marissa enjoys playing golf, building elaborate LEGO creations, and traveling to new places. Her home is in Indiana, where she's surrounded by corn and soybean fields. Visit her at marissashrock.com.

ALSO BY MARISSA SHROCK

The Georgia Rae Winston Mystery Series

Deadly Harvest

Deadly Holiday

Deadly Heritage

Deadly Harmony

Deadly Hideaway

The Emancipation Warriors Series

The First Principle

The Liberation

The Pursuit

The Agitator: A Novella

ACKNOWLEDGMENTS

I'd like to thank all the people who helped make this story possible. Thanks, Ryan Riggs for letting me tag along in the combine cab during harvest and giving me insight into the farming profession. Thank you, Trent Shrock for answering my farming questions.

Thanks to my beta readers, Julie Woodall, Bekah Shaffer, and Katie Briggs.

Thanks, Mom and Dad for being my story's very first readers and for your love, support, and encouragement.

Editing by A Little Red Ink

Cover Art by Seedlings Design Studio

Marketing Copy by JR2 Marketing & Advertising

Cimelia Press Logo by Race Point

www.ingramcontent.com/pod-product-compliance
Lightning Source LLC
Chambersburg PA
CBHW061140170626
46809CB00003B/933